4 Beekman

by Ron Clark

A SAMUEL FRENCH ACTING EDITION

SAMUEL FRENCH

FOUNDED 1830

NEW YORK HOLLYWOOD LONDON TORONTO

SAMUELFRENCH.COM

ISBN 978-0-573-65079-6   Printed in U.S.A.   #7960

MUSIC USE NOTE

Licensees are solely responsible for obtaining formal written permission from copyright owners to use copyrighted music in the performance of this play and are strongly cautioned to do so. If no such permission is obtained by the licensee, then the licensee must use only original music that the licensee owns and controls. Licensees are solely responsible and liable for all music clearances and shall indemnify the copyright owners of the play and their licensing agent, Samuel French, Inc., against any costs, expenses, losses and liabilities arising from the use of music by licensees.

IMPORTANT BILLING AND CREDIT REQUIREMENTS

All producers of *4 BEEKMAN must* give credit to the Author of the Play in all programs distributed in connection with performances of the Play, and in all instances in which the title of the Play appears for the purposes of advertising, publicizing or otherwise exploiting the Play and/or a production. The name of the Author *must* appear on a separate line on which no other name appears, immediately following the title and *must* appear in size of type not less than fifty percent of the size of the title type.

In addition the following credit must be given in all programs and publicity information distributed in association with this piece:

Music and Lyrics written by Ron Clark,
Augustus Music Publishing

CHARACTERS

(in order of appearance)

DEANNE PETRIDGE

ROBERT PETRIDGE

IINTERCOM VOICE

BORIS

LOUELLA HARTLEY

SKIP DAY

JEANNINE

JOVAN

INGA

AVI KAPLAN

GINA

MR. CHIU

SETTING

The play takes place in the Living Room of an upscale apartment in Manhattan. The time is the present.

ACT I

Scene 1

(MUSIC CUE #1. The large living room is empty. There is no furniture, no carpeting and nothing on the walls. Upstage is the front door. Doors to a large closet are stage right, next to front door. Stage left also has a door. It leads to guest bathroom. Downstage right is a hallway leading to O.S. Dining room, kitchen, master bedroom, guest rooms and more bathrooms. We hear the sound of laughter and jiggling of keys emanating from the other side of front door.)

DEANNE *(O.S., giggling)* Where are we? What are you doing?

ROBERT *(O.S.)* Just hold tight, darling. I believe this is the correct key.

(Sound of key in door. The front door opens as ROBERT PETRIDGE ENTERS carrying his new bride over the threshold. ROBERT is British and has the accent to prove it. He's in his mid to late fifties, handsome, greying at the temples, wearing a conservative suit. ROBERT is on the

serious side. He's a little tentative as he staggers in with her. DEANNE DAY PETRIDGE, wearing a blindfold over her eyes, is in her early thirties, American and quite attractive.

DEANNE. *(Trying to remove her blindfold.)* Hurry, I want to see.

(ROBERT deposits her gently on her feet then staggers some more and breathes deeply.)

DEANNE. *(CONT'D)* Are you Alright?
ROBERT. *(Catching his breath.)* I'm fine, darling, I'm fine.

(He regains his balance, helps her remove her blindfold. She looks around, excitedly. Goes to "windows" downstage.)

DEANNE. I love it! I just love it! It's so big and airy.
ROBERT. The furniture was supposed to be here by now. I called the storage place yesterday from Tahiti. I'm terribly sorry. I apologize for that.
DEANNE. *(Indicates stage left door.)* What's in there?
ROBERT. *(As he follows her.)* I believe that's the guest bathroom.

(DEANNE opens door, looks in.)

DEANNE. Nice.
(She walks by him, strokes his cheek, on her way to hallway, downstage right.)

ROBERT. I hope you're not angry at me for cutting our honeymoon short.

DEANNE. That's what I get for marrying...

(She's disappeared into hallway.)

DEANNE. *(CONT'D, O.S.)*...a high profile businessman.

ROBERT. *(Calls out to her.)* I apologize for that! Not for being a high profile businessman...The master bedroom is at the end of the hallway! How do you like the size of the kitchen? Pretty substantial for a New York apartment, wouldn't you say? There's also a delightful room for your studio! *(To himself.)* Assuming you still want to go on with your work. *(Resumes calling out to her.)* And there's another room for the little one when the time comes!

(As ROBERT starts toward hallway to join her, DEANNE returns. She's ashen.)

DEANNE. Where are we?

ROBERT. *(Confused)* What do you mean?

DEANNE. What street are we on?

ROBERT. Beekman, Beekman Place.

DEANNE. *(Looking for a place to sit.)* What address?

ROBERT. Four. Why?

DEANNE. *(As she sits on floor.)* Four, Beekman?

ROBERT. *(As he kneels down, next to her.)* It's a premium address. It's a marvellous building. What about that river view from the master bedroom? Surely, you like *that.*

DEANNE. What floor are we on?

ROBERT. Twenty second, why?

DEANNE. Is this apartment 22A?
ROBERT. I believe it is.

(ROBERT rushes to front door, opens it, goes out to corridor, returns, closes door and nods sheepishly.)

DEANNE. We're going to have to move.
ROBERT. We haven't even moved in yet.
DEANNE. Good. It'll make it easier.
ROBERT. What are you talking about, darling? I thought you'd love this apartment.
DEANNE. I do.
ROBERT. Then what's the problem?
DEANNE. *(Exhales deeply.)* This is where I lived with Skip.
ROBERT. Who's Skip?
DEANNE. Thomas, Skip, Day, my husband.
ROBERT. *I'm* your husband.
DEANNE. My ex.
ROBERT. I never heard you refer to him as Skip.
DEANNE. *Everybody* called him Skip
ROBERT. *I* didn't.
DEANNE. Everybody who knew him. He hated the way Thomas Day sounded. He said it sounded like some sort of yoga prayer. *(Says it very quickly.)* ThomasDay. *(As she gets up.)* We're moving.
ROBERT. Don't be ridiculous, darling *(With exaggerated enthusiasm.)* It'll be wonderful. I'll bet you'll feel right at horne when your furniture arrives.
DEANNE. I'm sure I will, and that's precisely why I can't stay here. *(A beat.)* Didn't you recognize the name when

you signed the papers?

ROBERT. I didn't pay any attention. My real estate brokers took care of all that. I don't even remember meeting the man. If that picture hadn't slipped out of your purse going through customs I still wouldn't know what he looks like.

DEANNE. That was an accident. It was stuck to the back of my MOMA card.

ROBERT. What about you? Didn't you recognize *my* name on the deed?

DEANNE. I left it to Skip to take care of everything. That was our arrangement. I got all the furniture...except for that stupid piano of his...and he got to handle the sale.

ROBERT. Well, he did a masterful job. Didn't you once tell me what an inept businessman he was? He sure wasn't in this case. You know he refused to corne down a single penny from his asking price.

DEANNE. I'll reimburse you for my part of the sale.

(Sound of INTERCOM buzzing.)

ROBERT. That won't be necessary, darling.

(He rushes to intercom on wall, next to front door.)

ROBERT. *(CONT'D, into intercom.)* Yes?

(The INTERCOM VOICE belongs to a gentleman of German extraction with matching accent.)
INTERCOM VOICE. Your furniture is here.

ROBERT. Oh good, send them right up. *(Hangs up, returns to DEANNE.)* They're here. I can't wait to see it. Did you have any of it at your mother's?

DEANNE. No, it was all in storage.

ROBERT. Let's hope it all fits.

DEANNE Of course it'll fit. It was here before.

ROBERT. Yes, that's right, what am I saying?

DEANNE. I should have known he'd pull something like this. The whole thing is so...it's so...Skip. He's an immature, callow, infantile baby.

ROBERT *(Trying to lighten the moment.)* Most babies are infantile.

DEANNE. Don't make fun of me.

ROBERT. I'm not. *(Holds her hands.)* I just want us to be happy in our new home. I swear, Dee, I'll make you forget you ever lived here and I'll make you forget he ever existed.

DEANNE. He *doesn't* exist. Unfortunately he *is* alive.

ROBERT. Ah, don't talk like that, darling. What's done is done and what is, is. Give it a month, please? For me? If you're not happy after a month we'll move into the Carlyle. You liked my apartment there, didn't you?

DEANNE. I told you I don't like living in hotels. That's why I moved in with my mother after the divorce.

ROBERT. *(Jokingly)* And I thought you did it to take care of your Mum.

(A slight smile crosses her lips.)

ROBERT. *(CONT'D)* One month, that's all I ask.

(She stares at him.)

ROBERT. *(CONT'D)* A week? A day.

DEANNE. *(Relinquishes)* Okay, one day.
ROBERT. And one night.

(He embraces her. DOORBELL.)

ROBERT. *(CONT'D)* Coming!

(He opens front door. Standing there is BORIS, the mover. A husky, slightly overweight man in his early twenties. He speaks with a Russian accent. BORIS likes to use American slang.)

BORIS. What a bummer! Partner not show up today. They say they send replacement. They lie. One king-size mattress coming in!

(He rolls in a large upright mattress on a dolly.)

ROBERT. Where's the bed frame?
BORIS. Maybe in next load. *(Indicates hallway.)* Bedroom?
ROBERT. Yes.
DEANNE. No, wait a minute. Put it in here, please.
ROBERT. But this is the living room.
DEANNE. Sorry, but I'm not sleeping in that room.
ROBERT. *(A little embarrassed.)* What are you saying?
DEANNE. I don't want the bed in the bedroom.

(BORIS doesn't quite know what to do. He just stands there waiting for his instructions.)

ROBERT. Why don't we let this nice young man put the mattress in the bedroom for now and you and I can discuss it later.

DEANNE. There's no discussing.

ROBERT. *(To BORIS.)* Why don't you put the mattress in here for now?

BORIS. Very smart. Never argue with daughter.

ROBERT. But she's not my...

BORIS. *(Interrupting)* Please, you help Boris?

(He motions to ROBERT to grab one end of the mattress as he grabs the other end.)

BORIS. *(CONT'D, to DEANNE.)* Where we put?

DEANNE. How about over here?

(ROBERT and BORIS tilt mattress and maneuver it toward stage left wall.)

DEANNE. *(CONT'D)* No, maybe it's better over here.

(She indicates stage right wall. ROBERT and BORIS struggle with the large mattress. They place it on the floor, stage right, next to hallway.)

DEANNE. *(CONT'D)* That's good, right there.

BORIS. I go get more.

(He EXITS, pulling empty dolly. Closes door.)

ROBERT. Don't you think you're being a little...?

DEANNE. I'm not being a little. I just don't want to be reminded of Thomas.

ROBERT. I thought everybody called him Skip.

DEANNE. Not when you're mad at him.

ROBERT. How can you still be mad at him? You've been divorced for two years.

DEANNE. Three.

ROBERT. How is it going to look, having our bedroom in here and our living room in there?

DEANNE. *(Playfully)* It's going to look 'different'.

ROBERT. I suppose that's what I get for marrying someone half my age.

DEANNE. You're right. That's what you get...and a lot more.

(She kisses him on the cheek, then walks around the room figuring out where the furniture might go.)

ROBERT. I was thinking, once the furniture's all here, you and I might want to, as you say, 'grab a bite' with the Talbots this evening.

DEANNE. Please, not the Talbots.

ROBERT. I thought you liked them.

DEANNE. They're so *old.*

ROBERT. They're my age.

DEANNE. *(Quickly)* I mean in attitude. All they do is talk money.

ROBERT. Well, they're both bankers...

(DOORBELL. Robert quickly goes to door and opens it.
BORIS now has a sofa on his dolly. He starts in with it.)

BORIS. Where you want this?

DEANNE. You can take it through there into the master bedroom...I mean the living room.

BORIS. *(Gives her a thumbs-up.)* Hip and happening.

(He rolls dolly into hallway and out of view.
Sound of CELL PHONE. DEANNE and ROBERT each reach for their phone. It's ROBERT'S.)

ROBERT. *(Into phone.)* Petridge here...Already? I thought his flight wasn't due until late tonigh...I'll be right over. *(Hangs up.)* I'm afraid I have to hop over to the office for a little while. It's that Chinese chap I was telling you about. You know, the potential mega China deal?

DEANNE. You mean the one who cut short our honeymoon?

ROBERT. I'm terribly sorry, darling. I apologize for that.

DEANNE. I'm kidding.

ROBERT. It seems the chap came in a day early. You're not angry, are you?

DEANNE. Of course not.

ROBERT. I'll be back as soon as I can. I'm terribly sorry. I apologize.

(Kisses her on the cheek and EXITS.)

DEANNE. *(To the heavens.)* Please stop apologizing!
(She walks around the room contemplating where her belongings will go. She opens the door to large closet next to front door then closes it. She retrieves her cell

phone and dials.)

DEANNE. *(Into phone.)* Avi Kaplan, please...Who's this?
...Oh, you're the new receptionist...Well, tell him it's Deanne
and that I'm back...Avi!...Thank you, thank you very much...
what can I say? He didn't want a big wedding. He's been a
bachelor his whole life. He doesn't know from weddings...

(BORIS returns with empty dolly.)

BORIS. Excuse please?
DEANNE. *(Into phone.)* Can you hold on a second,
Avi?
BORIS. I place sofa so you see river. From bed you
would see even better.

(He EXITS with the empty dolly.)

DEANNE. Don't shut the door.

(BORIS shuts the door.)

DEANNE. *(CONT'D, back to phone.)* Sorry, Avi...Yes,
I'm back a few days early but I'd like to use those few days
to settle in...No, please don't send Jovan over. Besides you
don't have my new address...How did you know I was back
in my old apartment? *(Incredulous)* Skip Day called you!!!
(Stunned) That man is impossible!...Avi, I'm not ready to
work yet...Avi?...Avi?...*(She hangs up, discouraged. She
holds her head in her hands.)* Do I need this?

(DOORBELL)

DEANNE. *(CONT'D, as she goes to door, annoyed.)*
Please leave the door open next time.

*(She opens door. It's not BORIS, it's her mother, LOUELLA.
LOUELLA is a handsome woman in her fifties, full
of energy and a bit of a scatter brain. She holds a gift
wrapped box.)*

DEANNE. *(CONT'D, surprised.)* Mother!

(LOUELLA ENTERS. DEANNE leaves the door ajar.)

LOUELLA. I swear to God, I'm never going on a cruise
again. I was the only one on board without a walker. And that
included the captain.
DEANNE. How did you know where I was? Don't tell
me, Skip?

(LOUELLA nods as she presents DEANNE with the gift box.)

LOUELLA. Didn't the two of you live somewhere in this
area before? *(She goes to windows and looks out.)*
DEANNE. Yes, *exactly* in this area.
LOUELLA. Was it the building across the street?
DEANNE. *(Trying to be very patient.)* No.
LOUELLA. Was it the building next door?
DEANNE. No.
LOUELLA. Don't tell me it was *this* building.
DEANNE. Okay, I won't tell you it was this building.

LOUELLA. It was, wasn't it? How crazy is *that? (Hesitantly)* Was it on the same floor?
DEANNE. Yes.
LOUELLA. The same apartment?

(She jumps up and down with excitement.)

DEANNE. You're not on a Game Show, Mother. Yes, it's the exact same *floor and* the *exact* same *apartment.*
LOUELLA. How do you like that!
DEANNE. I don't.

(DEANNE is opening LOUELLA'S gift.)

LOUELLA. So how was Fiji?
DEANNE. *(Correcting her.)* Tahiti.
LOUELLA. Who cares? As long as they have Mai Tais.

(DEANNE has opened the gift.)

DEANNE. Bagels?
LOUELLA. Yes, from H & H Bagels. You don't have that on the East Side. *(Looks around.)* Where's your new husband? I just realized something. Your new husband is older than your old husband. *(Laughs)*
DEANNE. Mother, don't start.
LOUELLA. I'll bet, had your father not run out on us when you were two, your need for a father figure would have been greatly diminished.
DEANNE. And I'll bet, had you not taken that Pseudo Psychology class at The New School your need to butt in

would have been totally eliminated.

LOUELLA. *(Notices mattress.)* How quaint. Reminds me of my hippie days. I suppose this was *his* idea. The moment he comes in from work he can jump right into bed with you.

DEANNE. Mother!

LOUELLA. Pretty good for an old guy.

DEANNE. He's *not* an old guy. He's a year younger than *you*, for heaven's sake.

LOUELLA. Personally, I've always preferred younger men.

DEANNE. I know, but did you have to marry all of them?

LOUELLA. I only married three. Not counting your father, of course. Wasn't Skip younger than you?

DEANNE. By a month.

LOUELLA. Well, it's a start. *(Looks at her watch.)* I really should be going. I have matinee tickets to some new Mamet play. *(A beat.)* Do you think they use that language in the afternoon?

DEANNE. *(Stares at her mother.)* How did you get past the doorman downstairs?

LOUELLA. It wasn't easy. I told him he reminded me of the son I never had. Then I clicked my heels and saluted him.

(KNOCK at door.)

DEANNE. *(Calls off.)* You don't have to knock each time.

(Door pushes open. BORIS is there with several lamps and a

dressmaker's 'female-form' mannequin on his dolly.)

BORIS. *(Indicates mannequin.)* Where do you want hot babe to sleep?

DEANNE. You can put that in the back room.

BORIS. And this? *(Indicates lamps.)* Here or living room? *(Points to stage right hallway.)*

DEANNE. You can leave them in here, one on each side of the *bed.*

(BORIS places lamps on each side of mattress.)

LOUELLA. Aren't you going to introduce us?

DEANNE. Boris, this is my mother. Mother, this is Boris.

BORIS. Pleasure. I already meet father.

(LOUELLA stifles a laugh. BORIS grabs the mannequin and EXITS through stage right hallway.)

LOUELLA. Let me get this straight. This is going to be your permanent bedroom?

DEANNE. That's right.

LOUELLA. Because?

DEANNE. Because it's none of your business.

(There's a KNOCK at the door and it opens slowly. Standing there is SKIP DAY, bouquet of flowers in hand. SKIP is in his late thirties, good looking, casually dressed and somewhat immature.)

SKIP. It's your Neighborhood Welcome Wagon! Without the wagon but with some marked down roses instead.

LOUELLA. Hey, if it isn't husband number one!

SKIP. Hi Mrs. Hartley. Still playing the ponies?

LOUELLA. Only when they're running. Unfortunately, the ones I bet on tend to stroll. *(Shares laugh with SKIP.)*

DEANNE. *(Confused, to SKIP.)* What are *you* doing here?

SKIP. I was in the neighborhood and I thought I'd come by, see how the honeymoon went, see if you're still married, see if you like your new home.

(BORIS walks back in, notices SKIP.)

BORIS. *(To DEANNE.)* This your bro?

SKIP. Close enough.

BORIS. *(Impressed)* Very cool family. I be right back.

(He EXITS with the empty dolly.)

DEANNE. *(To SKIP.)* How could you?

SKIP. How could I what?

LOUELLA. Yeah, how could he what?

DEANNE. Mother, please! *(To SKIP.)* How could you sell this place to my husband knowing full well that he was my husband?

SKIP. You're the one who said I could handle everything. Besides, he made us an offer I couldn't refuse.

LOUELLA. How much?

DEANNE. Mother! *(To SKIP.)* You put me in a terrible position.

SKIP. Aren't you going to take my flowers?

LOUELLA. Yes, take the flowers, dear.

(DEANNE gives her mother a dirty look and reluctantly takes flowers.)

LOUELLA. *(CONT'D, staring at the two of them.)* I always liked the way you two looked together.

(DEANNE steps away from SKIP and searches for something to put flowers in.)

DEANNE. I have nothing to put them in. Here, take them back. *(Shoving flowers back in his hands.)*

SKIP. You know what my mother used to do when she got flowers from my dad? Which was very rarely.

DEANNE. You're not putting them in the toilet bowl.

SKIP. Why not? They'll keep for days. *(He makes his way to guest bathroom and continues speaking O.S.)* Providing you use the other bathrooms, of course.

LOUELLA. He's so youthful, don't you think?

DEANNE. Adolescent is more like it.

SKIP. *(Returns)* Don't you just love the layout of this apartment? To tell you the truth I was sorry we decided to sell it.

DEANNE. Is that why you overcharged the poor man?

SKIP. *(Incredulous)* Poor man? *(A beat.)* Where is Bob, by the way?

DEANNE. It's not Bob, it's Robert.

LOUELLA. Yeah, what's the matter with you? Bob is not a name you give to an important businessman like Bob. You need a serious name like *Robert* when you're a serious person.

DEANNE. Robert is not serious. In fact he has a nifty sense of humor. It's just that he's a *mature* person. *(Pointedly, to SKIP.)* Not a *child.*

LOUELLA. *(To SKIP.)* How would you like to go see a Mamet play right now?

SKIP. They do Mamet in the afternoon?

LOUELLA. *(To DEANNE.)* See?

SKIP. Thanks, but I have things to do.

DEANNE. *(To LOUELLA.)* What happened to the person you were supposed to go with?

LOUELLA. I wasn't suppose to go with *anybody.*

DEANNE. Then why did you get two tickets?

LOUELLA. I always buy two tickets. You never know who you're going to run into.

SKIP. I admire your attitude Mrs. Hartley. I always did.

LOUELLA. Didn't you used to call me Louella?

SKIP. I used to call you 'Mom' but that was when I was your son-in-law.

LOUELLA. As far as I'm concerned you're *still* my son-in-law.

DEANNE. Are you two finished?

(The front door opens and in ENTERS BORIS with another load on his dolly.)

BORIS. One living room chair and one empty bird cage.

SKIP. *(Looks at DEANNE.)* The bird cage, huh?

DEANNE. I was going to throw it out but Robert told me he likes birds. He's thinking of getting us a parakeet.

SKIP. But you *hate* birds!

DEANNE. I don't *hate* birds. It's just that I like their cages better.

BORIS. I go place chair in living room. (*Pushes dolly toward hallway.*) I wing it with bird cage. *(Laughs as he EXITS.)* Wing it.

LOUELLA. *(To DEANNE.)* You have to admit, that was a pretty original way to give someone an engagement ring, nestled at the bottom of the feeder.

DEANNE. Yes, he was original...*(Turning to SKIP.)* if nothing else.

SKIP. I wrote pretty good songs too.

DEANNE. *(Reluctantly)* Sometimes.

LOUELLA. I liked his songs.

DEANNE. Mom, you're not in this.

SKIP. *(To DEANNE, lovingly.)* I wrote a pretty good one for *you.*

DEANNE. And then you went and sold it to that airline for a stupid TV commercial.

SKIP. It got us this apartment, didn't it?

LOUELLA. I loved the one you wrote for Volvo and the one you wrote for Gillette and the one you came up with for Dove soap. How did it go again?
(Sings)
I CANNOT LIVE WITHOUT YOU,
COME SHARE MY LOVE
I NEED YOU NOW,
COME SHARE MY DOVE...

DEANNE. Mother, please.

(BORIS returns with his empty dolly.)

BORIS. I put bird cage in baby's room. Be right back.

(He EXITS with dolly.)

SKIP & LOUELLA. *(In unison.)* Baby's room?

DEANNE. He's just assuming.

LOUELLA. Who, Robert?

DEANNE. No, Boris.

SKIP. Who's Boris?

LOUELLA. The mover.

SKIP. *(To DEANNE.)* Are you pregnant? Is that why you had to marry Robert so fast?

DEANNE. How dare you? And what if I was pregnant? What's it to you?

SKIP. Well, I'd like to know if there's going to be a baby crying next door.

DEANNE. *(Stunned)* What did you just say?

SKIP. I said...

DEANNE. I know what you said, but what did you say?

SKIP. *(Timidly)* Well, with my half of the money I made from Mr. Petridge I was able to pay off my debts, put a few dollars aside for a rainy day and buy a smaller place next door. Mind you, I don't have a river view.

DEANNE. You know what you are? You're despicable. You're worse than despicable, you're...

SKIP. *(To LOUELLA)* There's something worse than despicable?

(LOUELLA shrugs.)

DEANNE. *(To SKIP.)* Get out! Get out, right now!

LOUELLA. You're not being very neighborly.

DEANNE. You too, out!

(Front door opens. JEANNINE, a very sexy French model-type, sticks her head in, followed by the rest of her body. She has flaming red hair and speaks with a French accent.
Please note: there are three sexy model-types in the play and could all be played by the same actress. The only difference is the clothing, the hair and the accent.)

JEANNINE. *(To SKIP.)* How am I supposed to learn to sing if you are not home to teach me how to sing? *(To LOUELLA.)* Are you, per chance, the ex?

LOUELLA. Thank you but no, *she* is.

(DEANNE looks at SKIP and just shakes her head.)

SKIP. Well, if you ever need anything...sugar, butter, bird seeds...You know where to find me.

JEANNINE. *(To DEANNE.)* A pleasure meeting you, madame. *(She EXITS with SKIP.)*

DEANNE. Did she just call me a madam?

LOUELLA. *(Confidentially)* Are you going to tell Robert that your ex lives nest door?

DEANNE. Out!

LOUELLA. You know where to find me also.

(She EXITS. DEANNE reaches for her cell phone and dials.)

DEANNE. *(On phone.)* This is Deanne Petridge...Thank you very much. Would you tell Mr. Petridge that his wife called and to please call her as soon as possible?

(Hangs up.
INTERCOM. An annoyed DEANNE goes to it.)

> DEANNE. *(CONT'D)* What?
> INTERCOM VOICE. A young man by the name of Joe Van is here to see you. Shall I send him up?
> DEANNE. It's Jovan and the answer is no. I mean, yes. Whatever.

(She hangs up. DOORBELL rings.)

> DEANNE. *(CONT'D)* So fast?

(She opens the door. It's BORIS. He ENTERS with another
load. This time his dolly holds several small tables.)

> BORIS. Where I put this?
> DEANNE. Who cares?
> BORIS. You don't want to see where Boris put things?
> DEANNE. *(Firmly)* No!
> BORIS. I am very sorry you have bad day. You know what Boris do when he have bad day? He drink cold beer. If you like I run to corner and bring back ice cold six-pack.
> DEANNE. That's very sweet of you, Boris but that won't be necessary. What a nice gesture. I mean...
> BORIS. *(Raises hand to stop her.)* Chill.

(He EXITS through stage right hallway.
MUSIC CUE #2.

Sound of PIANO and female VOICE doing the scales can be heard O.S. These sounds continue faintly throughout the following.)

DEANNE. What have I done to deserve this?

DOORBELL. She turns and starts toward partially open door. It pushes open slowly. Jovan, a nineteen year old Jamaican who is all gay-energy, runs over to Deanne and kisses her on both cheeks. He's holding a large envelope. He speaks with a Jamaican accent.

JOVAN. Welcome home, Mrs. Petridge.

DEANNE. It's okay, you can still call me Deanne.

JOVAN. We all missed you so much, Deanne. Mr. Kaplan was going crazy with you gone away like that.

DEANNE. I was only gone two weeks. Less than two weeks.

JOVAN. Two weeks without your sketches, the House of Kaplan almost became the House of Cards.

DEANNE. But I left a bunch of designs before I went away.

JOVAN. Apparently they were stolen.

DEANNE. What?

JOVAN. Yes, and they know who *did* it.

(DEANNE looks at JOVAN inquisitively.)

JOVAN. *(CONT'D)* Mrs. Kaplan. You see, the Kaplans are in the middle of a nasty divorce. She wants to start her own place and compete with him. It's driving him crazy. I can't take it anymore.

DEANNE. You shouldn't let it get to you, Jovan. It's not

your problem.

JOVAN. It is my problem when I am asked to choose sides.

DEANNE. What do you mean?

JOVAN. She is offering me employment. And she wants to give me more money.

DEANNE. So, is that what you're going to do?

JOVAN. If I go work for her then I will not be working with you anymore. Unless, of course, you decide to go work for her also.

DEANNE. I can't do that, Jovan. Avi Kaplan's been good to me. He lets me work at home. He lets me take time off to get married.

JOVAN. How frequently do you do that?

DEANNE. Twice. But that's not the point. He's already told me he's going to give me all the time off I want, to have a baby.

JOVAN. You are having a baby?

DEANNE. Well, eventually. Besides I don't like switching around. I don't like changes.

JOVAN. *(As he walks around, looks out at window.)* Is that why you are living in the exact same apartment you did when you were married to Skippy?

DEANNE. *(Laughs)* If he heard you call him that.

JOVAN. *(Suddenly realizing there's piano and singing in the b.g.)* You have a vocal teacher next door?

DEANNE. Let's put it this way. Something is being taught next door. We're not sure what exactly.

JOVAN. *(A beat.)* That is too complicated for my head. *(Back to business.)* So what do you suggest I do concerning my situation?

(BORIS appears from hallway with his empty dolly.)

BORIS. *(To JOVAN.)* Are you replacement for missing partner?

JOVAN. *(Disappointed)* Oh, you have a partner?

DEANNE. *(Coming to the rescue.)* He means a partner on his truck.

JOVAN. *(Impressed)* Oh, you have a truck?

DEANNE. Jovan, let the man work. Go ahead, Boris. Just bring up some more things.

(BORIS starts to go.)

JOVAN. Hurry back!

(BORIS EXITS.)

DEANNE. Stop that. The guy is totally straight.

JOVAN. So was I, once.

DEANNE. I don't believe you.

JOVAN. You're right. *(Beat)* Oh, I almost forgot. *(Hands her envelope.)* These are some of your old sketches. Mr. Kaplan believes the skirts should be significantly shorter.

DEANNE. Mr. Kaplan believes all skirts should be shorter. *(Opens envelope, looks at content.)*

JOVAN. He says, this season, he wants to 'corner' the youth market.

DEANNE. Yeah, the way he corners his secretaries?

JOVAN. You know me...*(Covering his eyes then his ears.)* See no evil, hear no evil.

DEANNE. *(Takes the sketches from him.)* I'll see what I can do.

JOVAN. I have also included a few of my own in there. Did I mention to you that I may be doing the costumes for an off-off-off Broadway production?

DEANNE. That's fabulous. How off is it?

JOVAN. It's in New Jersey. The southern tip of New Jersey.

DEANNE. So what? It's a start.

JOVAN. I would appreciate your opinion on the sketches.

DEANNE. Sure, I'll look them over.

JOVAN. Maybe some weekend you and your new husband can drive down to see the show. I'll get you, what they call 'comps'. It will be like a second honeymoon for you. Ciao!

(He EXITS. The music and singing has stopped next door. CELL PHONE rings.)

DEANNE. Hello...Oh hi, Robert. I'm glad you called. There's something you should know about our neighbor next door...You what?...I don't think so, Robert. The mover is still here and I want to start putting things away. Maybe I can meet Mr.Chiu some other time. We'll have him over for saki...You're right, I forgot, he's Chinese...No, you go ahead and have yourself a wonderful dinner. We'll talk later. See you when you get home...I love you too. Bye.

(Hangs up.
KNOCK on door. BORIS ENTERS with another load. This time the dolly supports a large flat TV screen and a number of large cardboard boxes.)

DEANNE. *(Noticing boxes.)* Oh good, clothing and dishes.

BORIS. *(Looks around.)* Prince Charming still on the scene?

DEANNE. No, he left. I assure you he's harmless.

BORIS. You want TV here or in back room?

DEANNE. That's a good question. Mr. Petridge and I haven't really discussed that.

BORIS. You call husband Mister Petridge?

DEANNE. No, of course not. I'm just calling him that in front of you. *(Looks over boxes.)* This one is for the dining room. You can take it in there. I guess the TV can stay in here.

BORIS. Radical. Me and girlfriend have TV in bedroom also. Late at night, soft porn come in handy. *(Unloads screen and rests it against wall, opposite mattress.)* I got cousin who hook this up for you. I call him.

DEANNE. That won't be necessary. I'm sure my husband has someone.

BORIS. Is okay I use toilet?

DEANNE. Sure, go ahead.

(BORIS opens door to guest bathroom and starts to ENTER. He immediately steps out gain.)

BORIS. Whoa! Flowers growing in there. *(Shakes head.)* Only in America.

DEANNE. I forgot about that. Use one of the other ones.

(BORIS crosses and heads for hallway.)

BORIS. Cannot wait to tell my woman about that.

(He EXITS still shaking his head. There's a KNOCK at the front door, followed by it opening slowly. It's SKIP.)

SKIP. Anybody home?

DEANNE. Short lesson today?

SKIP. Well, you don't want to give them too much at first.

DEANNE. I'll bet.

SKIP. Believe it or not, Jeannine has a pretty good voice.

DEANNE. Why not? She has the lungs for it. Is this it from now on, you dropping in every half hour? I don't think Robert's going to be too thrilled with that.

SKIP. What about you?

DEANNE. Skip, are you crazy! Didn't your lawyer give you a copy of our divorce papers?

SKIP. Don't remind me. Biggest mistake I ever made.

DEANNE. *You* didn't make it, I divorced *you!*

SKIP. I'll be honest with you, Dee, I didn't think you'd go through with it. I also didn't think you'd marry again so fast.

DEANNE. I guess you didn't know me very well.

(BORIS RE-ENTERS, sees SKIP.)

BORIS. Oh, big brother back! Is nice when family pitch in. *(Retrieves his dolly. To DEANNE.)* Is okay I take break now? Maybe grab some lunch.

DEANNE. No, go ahead.

SKIP. I'll help my 'sister' unpack.

BORIS. *(To DEANNE.)* You lucky woman. I have brother don't do squat for me. *(He EXITS.)*

DEANNE. You are, without a doubt, the most impertinent, impudent, shameless, narcissistic person I have ever met.

SKIP. And yet you fell in love with me once.

DEANNE. You were different then.

SKIP. How so?

DEANNE. Well, for one thing, you had ambition when I met you. You were going to write the great American Musical, not those inane jingles for tooth paste whiteners.

SKIP. Maybe that's my calling in life. Besides, that's not why you left me.

DEANNE. It's one of the *many* reasons.

SKIP. It's more because I wasn't ready to have a child.

DEANNE. Why would you want a child? You *are* a child. God, you didn't even want to *talk* about it.

SKIP. What can I tell you, I don't think this is a fit world in which to raise children.

DEANNE. What if your parents had said that.

SKIP. My parents didn't say anything. they were Republicans.

DEANNE. Always the smart-ass comeback.

SKIP. Look, Dee, I'm not here to start trouble. I just want you to know that...I'm here for you.

DEANNE. *(Incredulous)* What?

SKIP. *(Awkwardly)* I don't mean here like *here...I* guess what I'm trying to say is, if you ever need me for *anything,* just knock on the wall. I'll be over before you can say...

DEANNE. Goodbye Skip.

(He starts to go as front door opens and in walks INGA, another model-type. This time she's a blonde and looks a lot like JEANNINE. INGA speaks with a Scandinavian accent.)

INGA. There you are. How is Inga supposed to learn piano if piano teacher missing?

(SKIP gives DEANNE an embarrassed look.)

SKIP. *(To INGA.)* How did you get upstairs?
INGA. The doorman fell in love with my boots.

(They EXIT. BORIS ENTERS without his dolly, looks back at INGA.)

BORIS. Your brother sure know how to pick'em. *(Beat)* Boris have bad news.
DEANNE. Some furniture's missing?
BORIS. No, no, everything cool. Well, maybe not so cool.
DEANNE. what is it?
BORIS. Water main on street bummed out. Have to move truck. I come back tomorrow morning. Maybe partner back then. Is good with you?
DEANNE. I don't think Mr. Petridge will be too happy.
BORIS. *(Glances at mattress.)* Not to worry. Mr. Petridge will be plenty happy. See you in AM.

(He EXITS, closing door behind him. DEANNE walks over to

one of the cardboard boxes and starts opening it.
MUSIC CUE #3.
Sound of bad PIANO playing next door. DEANNE reacts,
grasps her head with both hands.)

DEANNE. Oh, noooooooo!

END OF SCENE

Scene 2

(That night. The two boxes are no longer there. The mattress
now has sheets and a bedspread on it. The lamps, on
either side of bed, are on low. The guest bathroom door
opens and out steps ROBERT. He wears a silk bathrobe
over a pair of neatly pressed pajamas. He goes to right
side of the bed, removes his bathrobe, carefully folding
it. He then deposits it on the night table, He picks up a
copy of Business Week magazine, turns up his light and
gets into bed. A moment later, DEANNE ENTERS from
hallway, wearing a negligee under a sheer robe. As she
approaches bed, she slips off her robe.)

ROBERT. *(Looks at her and smiles.)* Maybe I won't read
tonight. *(Turns his light off and meticulously puts magazine*
away.)

DEANNE. *(As she gets into bed.)* Aren't you tired after
that four hour meal you had with Mr. Chiu?

ROBERT. You mean Sun Yun. We're on a first name basis
now. I can't wait for you to meet him. He's like me, he loves
the smell of a deal. The chaps at the club are going to like this

guy. You know, I'm beginning to think that communists make the best capitalists.

(MUSIC CUE #4.
Sound of PIANO playing from next door.)

> DEANNE. *(Reacting to piano.)* Oh, God.
> ROBERT. What's wrong?
> DEANNE. Don't you hear it?

(ROBERT listens. The piano is playing a beautiful, melodic ballad.)

> ROBERT. It's pretty. Sounds familiar.
> DEANNE. It sounds familiar because you heard it a thousand times on a television commercial.
> ROBERT. *(Doubtful)* A pretty song like that? They wouldn't turn it into a commercial.
> DEANNE. Is that so?
> *(Sings. Sample #5 on Disc.)*
> COME MEET THE WORLD,
> COME FLY AMERICAN...

> ROBERT. You're right. What a shame. You'd think the person who wrote that would do something more with it.

(The piano is getting louder.)

> DEANNE. *(Annoyed)* Is he going to play that thing all night?
> ROBERT. Is it really bothering you, darling?
> DEANNE. *(Firmly)* Yes!

ROBERT. I apologize for that. *(As he rises.)* I'll put an end to it.

DEANNE. What are you going to do?

(ROBERT goes to wall opposite their mattress and knocks three times. The music immediately stops.)

DEANNE. I wish you hadn't done that.

ROBERT. *(As he returns to bed.)* It worked.

(He gets back into bed and snuggles up to her.)

DEANNE. I'm really not in the mood now.

ROBERT. I understand. Forgive me. I apologize. *(Kisses her gently on the cheek then turns away.)* Goodnight, dear.

DEANNE. Goodnight.

(Reaches up and turns her light off. The room is dark. We can barely see the 'bed'. There's a KNOCK at the door.)

ROBERT. Who in the world would come by at this hour? And what happened to our doorman?

(Turns his light on and gets up.)

DEANNE. *(Jokingly)* Maybe it's Mr. Chiu. Maybe he threw some money at the doorman.

ROBERT. It can't be Sun Yun. *(As he makes his way to front door.)* Unless, of course, he's mixed up with the time change. *(At the door.)* Who is it?

SKIP. *(0. S.)* Your neighbor.

(DEANNE immediately gets up, grabs her robe and rushes to hallway.)

ROBERT. What are you doing?

(He opens front door as DEANNE disappears through hallway.)

SKIP. I just wanted to apologize for the piano. I didn't realize it was so late.

ROBERT. Come in, come in. *(Looking SKIP over.)* Have we met before?

SKIP. Well, sort of.

(SKIP ENTERS tentatively.)

ROBERT. *(Feeling obliged to explain the mattress.)* My wife and I are sleeping in here for a few days until...uh...until the rest of the furniture arrives. *(Keeps eyeing SKIP.)* Where would we have met? *(Suddenly)* Now I know who you are! You're the young man in my wife's wallet.

SKIP. I am?

ROBERT. That means that my wife was *your* wife. *(Calls out.)* Honey, it's your ex! *(To SKIP.)* Talk about a small world.

SKIP. I just wanted to say I'm sorry for the piano. I apologize.

ROBERT. I do that all day long, apologize. Terrible habit. *(Confidentially)* I think it's starting to get on Deanne's nerves.

SKIP. Well, I really should be going.

ROBERT. I understand you work for American Airlines.

SKIP. No, I don't work for them, I just wrote this one song for their advertising campaign.

ROBERT. Don't let anybody fool you, they're a good solid company. I was just reading about them in Business Week. They expect to break even in the next twenty years. *(A beat.)* So you live next door.

SKIP. I'm afraid so.

ROBERT. *(Inquisitively)* Let me ask you something. When you sold me this place were you already living next door?

SKIP. *(Uneasy)* I really should go and let you sleep. *(Starts toward door.)* I promise I won't play the piano after eleven at night. Or, if you prefer, ten *(At the door.)* Sorry I woke you. Goodnight.

(He EXITS. ROBERT closes the door and returns to bed.)

ROBERT. *(Calls out.)* You can come out now! The coast is clear! *(DEANNE RETURNS.)*

DEANNE. That's it, we're moving.

ROBERT. Why? Just because your ex happens to live next door?

DEANNE. Really, Robert, did you have to ask him in?

(They both get back into bed.)

ROBERT. Were you aware that he resided next door?

DEANNE. I heard a rumor earlier today.

ROBERT. The man must love this building. I mean, enough to want to move back in.

DEANNE. Can we go to sleep now?

ROBERT. Sure, sure. I'm sorry.

(Reaches up to turn light off. The stage is practically dark.)

ROBERT. *(CONT'D)* Well, goodnight, darling.
DEANNE. Goodnight, Robert.
ROBERT. *(A beat.)* So that's Skip.
DEANNE. *(Quietly correcting him.)* Thomas.

END OF SCENE

Scene 3

(The next day. The 'bed' has been made. The front door is slightly ajar. It opens. BORIS, the mover, is rolling in another load of furniture. This time his dolly holds several stuffed chairs, end tables, lamps, etc. He starts toward hallway and runs into DEANNE. She's all dressed, ready to go out.)

DEANNE. I hope you don't mind but I have things to do. We'll figure out where it all goes later. In the meantime, you just keep bringing the furniture up.
BORIS. S.P.C.A.
DEANNE. It's A.S.A.P.

(INTERCOM. DEANNE goes to it, picks it up.)

DEANNE. *(CONT 'D)* Yes?
INTERCOM VOICE. A Mr. Kaplan is here.

DEANNE. *(Surprised)* Here?

(BORIS starts to go but stays.)

INTERCOM VOICE. Yes, that's what I said, here in the lobby.

DEANNE. Send him up, I guess. *(Hangs up.)* What the hell is he doing here?

BORIS. You want Boris to stay in case trouble?

DEANNE. *(Laughs)* No, no. He's my boss. It's just that he's never come to my place before.

BORIS. I stay. Keep eyes on him.

DEANNE. That won't be necessary.

BORIS. Boris strong. Can pick up large heavy man and throw out window.

DEANNE. I'm sure you can but please...you go do what you have to do.

BORIS. No problem.

(He EXITS down hallway. DOORBELL. DEANE opens door. AVI KAPLAN, a high strung, balding mid-forties man, ENTERS, looks around, goes to window. He has a slight Isreali accent.)

AVI. Nice building. The doorman's a Nazi.

DEANNE. He's just a little overzealous.

AVI. Let me get right to the point. There's trouble in the garment district. To be more specific, there's trouble at the House of Kaplan.

DEANNE. I heard.

AVI. It's out already?

DEANNE. It's not out. I just heard if from Jovan. He came by yesterday.

AVI. That traitor.

DEANNE. Don't tell me he went to work for your wife.

AVI. Not yet but I know he's thinking about it. She already approached two of my best cutters. She's offering them almost twice what I pay them.

DEANNE. How can she afford that?

AVI. She's planning to milk me for every cent I've got.

(BORIS re-appears, pulling his empty dolly.)

AVI. *(CONT'D)* Is this the new husband?

DEANNE. *(Laughs)* No, this is Boris. He's moving us in.

BORIS. How you do?

(He shakes hands with AVI. AVI winces with pain.)

BORIS. *(CONT'D, to DEANNE.)* I bring up bathroom stuff. What bathroom I put in?

DEANNE. For now, put it in the one off the master bedroom. I'll deal with it later. *(He EXITS.)*

AVI. *(Looks around, notices mattress.)* If you have a master bedroom, what's this doing here?

DEANNE. It's a long story.

AVI. You're lucky. my story is short. A week ago my Millie and I were the happiest couple in Sheepshead Bay. Then she hits me with the news. She's already filed for divorce and she's setting up a business to go up against mine.

DEANNE. What are her grounds for divorce?

AVI. She says she caught me cheating with the receptionist one time too many.

DEANNE. Is that true?

AVI. Yes, but is that any reason to walk out on a happy marriage?

DEANNE. I'm the wrong person to ask.

AVI. Twenty two years I spent with that woman. How many years were you married?

DEANNE. Two.

AVI. So add twenty to that. *(Back to business.)* Here's what I need from you. *(DEANNE looks at AVI.)*

AVI. *(CONT'D)* I need you to talk to Manny, Moe and Jovan.

DEANNE. Who are Manny and Moe?

AVI. My cutters.

DEANNE. Why would they listen to *me?*

AVI. Because you're a woman. They're listening to Millie, maybe they'll listen to you.

DEANNE. What can I possibly offer them? I'm a dress designer I'm not the owner.

AVI. Offer them more money.

DEANNE. Why can't *you* do that?

AVI. I don't want to give them the satisfaction of knowing they've got me over a barrel.

DEANNE. This makes no sense whatsoever.

(KNOCK on door, followed by the door opening wide. It's SKIP. He spots AVI.)

SKIP. *(Rushing to AVI to shake his hand.)* Avi Kaplan! So nice to see you.

AVI. *(Confused, to DEANNE.)* What the hell's *he* doing here?

DEANNE. He's part of my long story.

SKIP. So, how have you been?

AVI. Lousy! And getting worse by the minute.

SKIP. You're not sick, are you?

AVI. Sick I could handle.

DEANNE. He's having marital problems.

SKIP. Welcome to the club.

DEANNE. What can I do for you, Skip?

SKIP. Oh, I almost forgot. I'm expecting a package and I have to go out. I was wondering if I could have it delivered here.

DEANNE. Why can't they leave it with the doorman?

SKIP. That Nazi!

AVI. *(To DEANNE.)* See?

DEANNE. But I'm not going to be here. I have to go out myself.

SKIP. But the mover's still here.

(Just then BORIS ENTERS with another load.)

BORIS. *(To SKIP, singing.)* WE ARE FA-MA-LY...

(He drags his dolly past them and heads for hallway.)

DEANNE. *(Relenting)* Okay, you can have the package sent up. *(Calls out.)* Boris, if a package comes for my 'brother' it's okay to leave it here!

AVI. Brother? I'm so confused.

(A third model-type shows up at the front door. GINA looks a

lot like the other two, only this one has jet black hair and speaks with an Italian accent.)

GINA. Maestro, how much longer am I supposed to wait for you?

SKIP. *(A little embarrassed.)* This is Gina.

DEANNE. How can you tell?

GINA. *(To SKIP, confused.)* What does she mean?

(AVI steps forward, extending his hand.)

AVI. Always a pleasure to meet a size 4.

GINA. Grazie.

SKIP. *(As he ushers GINA out.)* Good seeing you, Avi. You too, Dee.

(They EXIT.)

AVI. You live next door to your ex?

DEANNE. Not really. It's more like he lives next door to me.

AVI. *(Sarcastic)* That's much clearer.

DEANNE. Listen Avi, I was thinking maybe I could come work at the shop for awhile.

AVI. No room. I'm remodelling.

(BORIS APPEARS with his empty dolly and heads for front door.)

BORIS. Second bedroom filling up fast. Maybe I put next load in baby's room.

(AVI stares at DEANNE.)

DEANNE. Sure, whatever.

(BORIS EXITS.)

DEANNE. *(CONT'D)* What are you staring at?
AVI. That's *exactly* how Millie got me to marry her.
DEANNE. Well I'm not pregnant.
AVI. She wasn't either. She had just put on some weight.

(Sound of INTERCOM.)

DEANNE. Will you excuse me? *(Into intercom.)* Yes?
INTERCOM VOICE. Jovan is back. Says it's urgent.
AVI. *(Quietly)* Is there a service elevator?
DEANNE. *(Into intercom.)* Just a moment. *(Cups intercom, to AVI.)* Why won't you face Jovan?
AVI. I don't want him to know I'm here, wheeling and dealing.
DEANNE. Is that what you're doing?
AVI. Of course not. You know me better than that.
DEANNE. *(Into intercom.)* Send him up. *(Hangs up, to AVI.)* The service elevator is at the end of the corridor but the mover is using it.
AVI. I'll work something out with him. I got cash. *(As he rushes out the door.)* Come by after lunch and talk to my cutters, *please!*

(He EXITS. Cell phone RINGS. DEANNE flips it open and looks.)

DEANNE. *(Into phone, annoyed.)* Yes mother, what is it? ...Yes, Robert's at the office...No, Skip is not here.

(DOORBELL)

DEANNE. *(CONT'D, into phone, as she goes to door.)* ...No, that's not him.

(She opens the door. It's JOVAN.)

DEANNE. *(CONT'D, back to phone.)*...It's none of your business. Goodbye. *(Hangs up, to JOVAN.)* Come on in.

(He ENTERS.)

JOVAN. *(Referring to phone call.)* Your mother? *(DEANNE nods.)* I figured as much. I just saw a man run down the corridor who looked a lot like Mr. Kaplan,.

DEANNE. Really? *(Closes door behind him.)* So what brings you here this morning?

JOVAN. More gossip.

DEANNE. Now what?

JOVAN. Mrs. Kaplan ran off with one of the cutters.

DEANNE. Does Avi know?

JOVAN. It just happened.

DEANNE. Was it Manny?

JOVAN. No, Moe. Anyway, she showed up about an hour ago and dragged him away.

DEANNE. He didn't want to go?

JOVAN. Would you?

DEANNE. I don't think I ever met Mrs. Kaplan.

JOVAN. Of course you did. She's the one who shows up at every Christmas party dressed as Baby Jesus.

DEANNE. That's *her?* I thought Avi's wife was Jewish?

JOVAN. She is. She does it to drive him crazy.

DEANNE. What a couple!

JOVAN. So, have you decided to jump ship and join The House of Mrs. Kaplan?

DEANNE. First of all, she hasn't approached me and second of all, I wouldn't do that to Avi. He's always been good to me. Sure he doesn't pay me enough but he does let me work at home.

JOVAN. And that's important to you?

DEANNE. Yes it is.

(DOORBELL)

DEANNE. *(CONT'D)* Now what?

(She goes to door, opens it. It's BORIS with another load that includes a large armoire.)

JOVAN Well, well, well, if it isn't the man with the great big double parked truck! Good to see you, Boris.

DEANNE. You remembered his name?

(BORIS gets behind dolly and pushes the heavy load toward hallway.)

JOVAN. *(As he focusses on BORIS'S rear end.)* Jovan never forgets a face.

DEANNE. *(Calls out to BORIS as he moves off.)* You know you *can* sue for harassment!

(BORIS disappears.)

JOVAN. I think he's interested. I'd better go. I want to get back before Avi does. I don't want to miss the look on his face when he finds out that 'Moe is no mo'. Say goodbye to Mr. Buns. *(Starts to go, stops.)* Is it true what the doorman told me, that Skippy lives next door? *(Before she can answer.)* Tres French!

(He EXITS, leaving the door ajar. DEANNE heads for offstage rooms.)

DEANNE. *(Calls out.)* The armoire goes in the living room!

(She disappears. A moment later there's a knock at the front door. A second knock is followed by the door opening slowly as SKIP ENTERS tentatively.)

SKIP. *(Calling out.)* Anybody home?

(He stares at the mattress, shakes his head and smiles DEANNE reappears. She's taken aback at the sight of him.)

DEANNE. What are *you* doing here?
SKIP. I knocked and then I called out.
DEANNE. I was busy in the back with Boris.
SKIP. Boris?
DEANNE. The mover.
SKIP. He's still here? Who knew we owned so much stuff.
DEANNE. *We?* I got the furniture, remember?

SKIP. Oh yeah, sorry. *(A beat.)* I'll bet had you known you were moving back into this place you wouldn't have had to put it all in storage.

DEANNE. Well, I didn't know, did I?

SKIP. Sorry, I apologize.

DEANNE. Now you're starting to sound like Robert.

SKIP. Oh? Do I detect a little...?

DEANNE. You detect *nothing. (Starting to lose patience.)* Now, was there something you wanted to talk to me about?

SKIP. Yes, I suppose you could say that.

DEANNE. Never mind what *I* could say. What about you? What do you want to say?

SKIP. *(Hesitantly)* I know it sounds like I'm beating around the bush...

DEANNE. It doesn't sound like it, it *is* it. If you have something to say why don't you just come right out say it? That was always one of your many faults, Skip.

SKIP. Were there that many?

DEANNE. Yes, there were.

SKIP. What about my good qualities? Didn't they count?

DEANNE. Not when your faults outnumbered them ten to one.

SKIP. *(Astounded)* Ten to one?

DEANNE. Okay, five to one. That's still a tremendous disparity.

SKIP. Jeez, I would have thought three to one, tops.

DEANNE. Ten to one, three to one, what's the difference?

(BORIS walks by with his empty dolly.)

BORIS. If you bet on horse it makes big difference. I come back.

(He EXITS.)

SKIP. The reason I came by is that I've been doing some thinking, some serious thinking.

DEANNE. Well, that's something new.

SKIP. My selling this place to your husband and then moving next door was a lame attempt at holding on to you.

DEANNE. And the Bimbos, is that part of holding on to me?

SKIP. Oh, that's just me being immature again. They don't mean anything to me. It's just companionship. It gets lonely being a bachelor.

DEANNE. I'll bet.

SKIP. Besides, I have to make a living.

DEANNE. Oh, you're not earning enough with that Cadillac song that's on TV all day and all night? And what about that other one for Dove Soap? You're so clever the way you rhyme 'love' and 'Dove'. What a waste!

SKIP. You're right. I'm always taking the easy way out. I should've worked harder at my music. I should've worked harder at our marriage. I should've done a lot of things differently but the fact is, I miss you. I miss you very much. I really do.

DEANNE. It's a little late for all this, don't you think? *(Holds out her ring finger.)*

SKIP. Yes, I know, I know. *(Takes a deep breath then blurts it out.)* I came by to tell you that I put my place up for sale.

DEANNE. *(Surprised)* You did?

SKIP. I think it'll be better this way, don't you?

DEANNE. Yes, of course.

SKIP. I already have a prospective buyer.

DEANNE. You do?

SKIP. I don't think I can handle running into you on a daily basis, knowing you're married to someone else. So, for starters I'm going to stop dropping in like this.

(Starts to move away.)

DEANNE. What about your package?

SKIP. I spoke to Herr Doorman and he reluctantly agreed to hold it for me. *(Goes back to her.)* You know, Dee, I'm never going to stop loving you. I just won't see you, that's all.

(They are practically face to face.)

SKIP. *(CONT'D)* You have to believe me when I say this. I wish you all the luck in the world.

(He moves in closer to her.)

DEANNE. Damn you.

(She starts pounding his chest with her fists.)

DEANNE. *(CONT'D)* I hate you.

(The pounding slowly decreases as he holds her more tightly. He looks down at her. She looks up at him. They kiss and stay kissed. The front door opens slowly. It's ROBERT. He's about to say something but then decides to leave, pulling the door quietly back to where it was. DEANNE and SKIP come out of their kiss.)

SKIP. I don't know where that came from.

DEANNE. As long as it's not going anywhere else.

SKIP. *(Making his way toward front door.)* I imagine the sale will take at least a few weeks, maybe more. I'll do my best to avoid eye contact.

(SKIP is at the door.)

DEANNE. And lip contact.

(Skip smiles longingly as BORIS returns with another load. SKIP EXITS.)

BORIS. *(As he ENTERS pulling the dolly. To SKIP.)* My sister, she won't even *talk* to me.

END OF ACT ONE

4 Beekman

ACT II
Scene 1

(MUSIC CUE #6. Several days later. The room now has a lived-in appearance. Everything is in place. The mattress is now part of a real bed with proper frame and spread and pillows. The flat screen TV is up as are several paintings. There's a rug on the floor as well as more pieces of furniture. We hear voices outside the door. The door opens and in walks ROBERT accompanied by MR. SUN YUN CHIU, a well dressed Chinese businessman in his mid-forties. MR. CHIU speaks English rather well but with a Chinese accent. He is quite jovial.)

ROBERT. *(As he reaches in and turns on the light. He indicates for MR. CHIU to go in.)* After you.

MR. CHIU. I thank you. *(They ENTER.)*

ROBERT. *(Calls out.)* Deanne, darling, are you decent?

MR. CHIU. *(As he looks around, goes to window.)* Nice view of other buildings. *(Notices the bed.)* Oooh...Mr. Robert cannot wait when he comes home.

(Laughs knowingly as he mimics diving into bed.)

ROBERT. No, no, nothing like that. It's just that my wife has a thing...*(Making it up.)*...about not sleeping on the...west side of a building.

MR.CHIU. Smart woman. She likes East better. Far East even better. *(Laughs at his joke.)*

ROBERT. *(Having no choice but to laugh along.)* Yes, something like that. Can I offer you a drink?

MR.CHIU. Scotch, please. Single malt preferable.

ROBERT. I'm sure we can manage that. Shall we move into the living room?

(DOORBELL.
MR. CHIU is closer to front door.)

MR.CHIU. I get it.

(He goes to door, opens it. It's LOUELLA.)

MR.CHIU. *(CONT'D)* Ah, Missus Robert. So nice to meet you. *(Extends his hand.)*

LOUELLA. *(Shaking hands.)* Nice to meet you too. And you are...?

ROBERT. *(Rushing over to clarify the situation.)* That's not my wi...

MR.CHIU. *(Interrupting him.)* I'm so glad you marry someone your own age. I Hate men who marry trophy wife.

ROBERT. But she's not...

LOUELLA. *(Realizing what's going on, jumps in and plays along.)* Honey, who *is* this charming Asian?

ROBERT. *(Afraid to say the wrong thing.)* This is Mr. Chiu. He's the gentleman I've been dealing with on that *enormous* China venture.

MR.CHIU. *(To LOUELLA.)* You can call me Sun Yun. Or better still, just Sun, like in sunshine. What should I call you?

(LOUELLA looks at ROBERT for help.)

ROBERT. *(Feeling trapped but afraid to rock the boat.)* You can call her Deanne, since that's her name. I was just about to fix Mr. Chiu a drink. Would you like one, darling?

LOUELLA. Don't mind if I do, sweetheart.

(The three of them start toward hallway.)

MR.CHIU. *(Slyly, to LOUELLA, as they go by bed.)* I like your idea for placement of bed. Very imaginative.

LOUELLA. Thank you...I think. *(Shrugs her shoulders, unseen by MR. CHIU, then calls off to ROBERT.)* Make mine a martini, extra dry, straight up with a twist.

MR.CHIU. Oh, you like the twist? *(Does the 'twist'.)* Old American dance just arrived in my country.

(Dances some more, They disappear into offstage 'living room'...)

ROBERT. *(O.S.)* Would you like that on the rocks, Sun Yun?

MR.CHIU. *(O.S.)* No, thank you. Just a little ice. *(Laughs at his own joke.)*

(LOUELLA and ROBERT laugh. Muffled small talk continues O.S.

The front door opens and in walks DEANNE. She hears the sound of voices and laughter emanating O.S. She slowly moves toward hallway.)

DEANNE. *(Calls out.)* Robert?

(She disappears through hallway.)

LOUELLA. *(O.S.)* There you are!

MR.CHIU. *(O.S.)* Who's this?

LOUELLA. *(O.S.)* This is my daughter...Louella.

MR.CHIU. *(O.S.)* Oh, beautiful name for beautiful daughter. So glad to meet you before I go back to China next Monday.

ROBERT. (O.S.) This is Mr. Chiu, the gentleman I was telling you about.

MR.CHIU. *(O.S.)* You can call me Sun. Me, son, you, daughter. *(Laughs uproariously at his joke.)*

DEANNE. *(O.S.)* Mother, can I see you in the other room for a moment?

LOUELLA. *(O.S.)* We be right back. I mean, we'll be right back.

MR.CHIU. *(O.S.)* Hurry!

(DEANNE and LOUELLA ENTER bedroom. They speak in loud whispers as muffled dialogue continues O.S.)

DEANNE. Do you mind telling me what the hell is going on?

LOUELLA. I'm just trying to help your husband. It seems that Mr. Chiu is choosy. He doesn't like men who marry younger women.

DEANNE. Well, that's too damn bad, isn't it?

LOUELLA. If Mr. Chiu finds out it's liable to blow the whole deal. It's just for a few days. You heard him. He's leaving Monday.

DEANNE. And you expect me to play Robert's daughter while you play his wife??

LOUELLA. Just for a few days.

DEANNE. And what *if* Mr. *Chiu* finds out about our charade? How do you think that's going to help Robert's mega China deal?

LOUELLA. I don't have all the answers.

DEANNE. You don't have *any* answers.

(ROBERT and MR. CHIU ENTER.)

ROBERT. *(Enthusiastically)* Well, are we ready to go eat? Sun Yun says he's *in* the mood for Chinese.

MR.CHIU. I wonder why. *(Laughs uproariously.)*

ROBERT. *(To DEANNE.)* Why don't you join us too?

MR.CHIU. Yes, yes. The more the *merrier.* I pay.

ROBERT. And he promised not to order *it* too spicy for me.

DEANNE. I'm afraid I have some *homework* to do.

MR.CHIU. Oh, you go to college. That's good.

DEANNE. Yes, I'm getting my masters in *communications.*

LOUELLA. Maybe you could do your homework later.

DEANNE. I can't, but thanks anyway.

MR.CHIU. Ah, too bad. So nice to meet you.

(Shakes hand with DEANNE.)

ROBERT. *(As he opens front door, to DEANNE.)* You be a good girl now.

DEANNE. *(Annoyed)* Yes, *daddy.*

MR.CHIU. You are lucky parents to have such a wonderful daughter.

ROBERT. We sure are. *(To LOUELLA.)* Aren't we, darling?

LOUELLA. Yes, we sure are.

(LOUELLA blows DEANNE a kiss as the three of them EXIT.)

DEANNE. *(Frustrated)* Ughhh!

(She walks around the room, still furious at what ROBERT and her mother just put her through. She then goes to the wall opposite the bed, bangs on it three times and immediately regrets have done that.)

DEANNE. *(CONT'D)* Big mistake.

(She walks around some more. There's a knock at the door. DEANNE takes a deep breath and goes to the door, opens it.)

SKIP. Emergency?

DEANNE. Sort of.

SKIP. *(Big grin.)* Robert run out on you?

DEANNE. Yeah, in a way.

SKIP. Don't tell me there's another woman.

DEANNE. Yes, my mother. *(Quickly)* Only kidding. *(Sadly)* All three of them went out for Chinese food. *(Almost in tears.)* I *love* Chinese food.

SKIP. Who's the third person?

DEANNE. Mr. Chiu.

SKIP. Who's Mr. Chiu, the chef?

DEANNE. No, he's a big mucky-muck from China and Robert is trying to close the deal of the century with him.

SKIP. Why don't we get our own Chinese food?

DEANNE. Yeah, why don't we?

SKIP. *(Going to phone on the night table on ROBERT'S side of the bed.)* I'll call that place over on Second Avenue.

(He sits and starts dialing.)

DEANNE. *(As she EXITS through hallway.)* Don't forget the Vegetable Moo Shu!

SKIP. *(To self.)* How could I ever forget the Vegetable Moo Shu? We practically lived on that.

DEANNE. *(O.S.)* Want a beer?

SKIP. *(Still to self.)* And that. *(Calls out.)* Yes! *(Into phone.)* Hi, this is Mr. Day at 4 Beekman Place, Apartment 22a. I'd like a double order of Vegetable Moo Shu...an order of Kung Pao Shrimp...some steamed broccoli...Some rice. One brown, one white...*(Lights begin to FADE.)*

SKIP. *(CONT'D, quietly into phone as he looks in hallway's direction.)* Make that Apartment 22b.

(Lights FADE)

END OF SCENE

Scene 2

(Several days later. DEANNE is doing some yoga poses to a DVD on the TV screen. The INTERCOM buzzes.)

DEANNE. *(As she goes to it, discouraged.)* Not today. *(Into intercom.)* Yes?

INTERCOM VOICE. Your Mr. Kaplan is here again.

DEANNE. *(Incredulous)* On a Sunday?

AVI. *(O.S., through intercom.)* At least I didn't show up on the Sabbath.

INTERCOM VOICE. Did you hear that?

DEANNE. Alright, send him up.

(She hangs up, turns TV off, folds her yoga mat and puts it away. She quickly straightens out the bed covers and throws on a shawl.

DOORBELL.

She opens the door. Standing there is AVI and JOVAN.)

DEANNE. Both of you?

AVI. *(As he walks in quickly, followed by JOVAN.)* Big news.

JOVAN. Big.

DEANNE. Mrs. Kaplan's back?

AVI. No.

DEANNE. Moe's back?

AVI. No. Here's the situation. My lawyer's been working on this day and night. This is what he came up with. If I had a fifty fifty partner when Mrs. Kaplan filed for divorce she'd only be entitled to share in my half.

DEANNE. But you don't have a partner.

(AVI and JOVAN look at each other and smile.)

DEANNE. *(CONT'D)* Isn't that illegal?

AVI. Depends on the lawyer.

DEANNE. And you want me to be your partner?

AVI. No, I want you to meet my new partner.

JOVAN. How do you do?

DEANNE. *(To JOVAN.)* No offence... *(To AVI.)* but Jovan is a runner.

AVI. And a damn good one too.

JOVAN. Thank you, partner.

AVI. *(To DEANNE.)* Now, here's where you come in.

DEANNE. I'm sorry but I have my own baggage to contend with these days.

JOVAN. No, this is good.

AVI. The House of Kaplan and Associate...

JOVAN. That's me.

AVI ...have decided to give you a raise, of sorts.

DEANNE. How can you possibly give me more money now that you have less?

AVI. Who said anything about money? We're talking title here.

DEANNE. *(Sarcastic)* Like associate?

JOVAN. No, that's taken.

AVI. *(Proudly)* Vice-President in charge of Creativity.

DEANNE. Thanks but that won't be necessary.

AVI. Okay, how about Chairman of the Board?

DEANNE. There is no board.

JOVAN. It will look impressive on your door.

DEANNE. You mean the door to my studio back there? *(Indicates hallway.)*

AVI. Alright then, how about this? *(Emphasizing every word.)* You-get-to-work-at-home.

DEANNE. I work at home *now.*

AVI. You continue to work at home, *and* you get a small raise.

DEANNE. I'll take it. Now, if you don't mind, Sundays are kind of special with me. I like to read the Times, put on some music, do a little yoga, make myself a sandwich...

AVI. Sounds good. What kind of sandwich?

JOVAN. I do yoga with my new roommate. He loves down-dog. He likes to fetch the ball. *(Laughs)*

DEANNE. That's slightly different from the way I do it.

AVI. I don't believe in yoga. I believe in hard work and smart lawyers.

(MUSIC CUE #7. Sound of piano accompanied by a male voice singing the scales next door.)

AVI. *(CONT'D)* What's that?

DEANNE. (Angry) He's not supposed to teach on weekends.

(She goes over to wall and listens.)

JOVAN. *(To AVI.)* He's a vocal teacher, among other things.

DEANNE. *(At wall, puzzled.)* That sounds like Sun Yun Chiu.

AVI. *(To JOVAN.)* Sun Yun Chiu. Is that anything like

Rap?

DEANNE What the hell would he be doing with Skip? *(She starts for the door.)* Will you excuse me a minute?

(She opens door and EXITS, leaving the door slightly ajar.)

AVI. I don't get her sometimes.

JOVAN. So, do you think she's happy with our proposition?

AVI. *(Looks at JOVAN.) Our* proposition? *(Then realizing.)* Oh yeah, I forgot.

(The music and the singing next door has stopped. The front door opens and in walk ROBERT and LOUELLA, laughing.)

LOUELLA. You are so funny. *(Surprised to see AVI and JOVAN.)* Avi Kaplan, what are you doing here? And Jovan, so nice to see you again. *(Extends her hand and shakes both of theirs.)* I don't believe you've met Deanne's latest husband. This is Bob...I mean, Robert Petridge. Robert, this is Dee's boss, Avi Kaplan and Jovan who...

JOVAN. *(Finishes her sentence.)*...is now his partner.

LOUELLA. Is that so? Well, congratulations.

ROBERT. *(As he shakes hands with both of them.)* Delighted to meet you both.

LOUELLA. *(To AVI.)* Have you ever attended the Ballet?

JOVAN. *(Quickly)* I have.

LOUELLA. Well, we just saw the most inventive, avant-guard dance company from the Netherlands. I didn't understand a single step but I loved it.

ROBERT. Yes, it was most clever.

JOVAN. I wonder if my roommate likes Ballet. It hasn't come up yet.

LOUELLA. *(Looks around.)* Where's Deanne?

JOVAN. She ran next door.

ROBERT. Again?

AVI. Apparently she didn't like the singing that was wafting through the walls. I thought it was pretty good.

(DEANNE returns, notices ROBERT and her mother. She leaves door half open.)

DEANNE. You're back. How was it?

LOUELLA. Scrumptious. Wasn't it, Bob?

(DEANNE reacts to name.)

ROBERT. Yes, most clever.

JOVAN. I suppose we should be leaving about now.

AVI. Smart thinking. *(To LOUELLA.)* I know I've told you this before but I'll say it again. You've got yourself a hell of a daughter there. *(To ROBERT.)* And you've got yourself a hell of a wife. *(To DEANNE.)* See you down at the office.

DEANNE. No, you won't.

AVI. You're right, I forgot.

JOVAN. He forgets.

(As he ushers AVI out. They EXIT.)

ROBERT. I didn't know you saw your boss socially.

DEANNE. I don't. It was more of a business call.

LOUELLA. Trouble at the House of Kaplan?

DEANNE. And at the Kaplan house. So, the Ballet was fun?

LOUELLA. And so was lunch before. We had Dim Sum at Shun Lee's. You should have come with us.

DEANNE. You only had two tickets.

LOUELLA. That's true.

ROBERT. *(To DEANNE, with a slight edge.)* And how are things next door?

DEANNE. Full of surprises.

(MR. CHIU appears at the door, along with one of SKIP'S 'students', INGA.)

DEANNE. *(CONT'D)* There's one of them now.

MR.CHIU. *(To ROBERT.)* I thought I heard your voice. *(Notices LOUELLA.)* Oh, and the Missus too.

ROBERT. *(Confused)* I was under the impression that you'd returned to China.

MR.CHIU. I was supposed to but last Friday I stop at Karaoke Bar and meet Inga. *(Doing the introductions.)* Inga, this is Mr. Mrs. Petridge, parents of beautiful daughter.

(DEANNE cringes.)

ROBERT. Actually, she's not really my...

MR.CHIU. *(Interrupting him.)* So we sing together all night and then she tells me how Mr. Skip is writing big wonderful Musical. I meet Mr. Skip, I listen, I like, I decide to invest.

LOUELLA. Does that mean you're no longer interested

in Robert's business venture?

MR.CHIU No, Sun Yun have plenty money. Invest in everything. Right, Inga?

(She giggles.)

ROBERT. You know, Sun, I haven't been totally honest with you.

MR.CHIU. Who is honest in business?

LOUELLA. *(Out of the side of her mouth, to ROBERT.)* Do you think this is the right time?

ROBERT. What I'm trying to say is...

DEANNE. I'm not sure I want to be here for this. *(She moves away.)*

ROBERT. *(Motions 'it's okay' to LOUELLA and DEANNE.)* The truth is, Deanna is not my wife. That is to say...

MR.CHIU. *(Interrupting)* So what? So you're shacking up.

ROBERT. No, no, you don't understand. *(Indicates LOUELLA and himself.)* We're not married and *her* name is Louella. *(Indicates DEANNE and himself.)* But *we are,* and *her* name is Deanne.

MR.CHIU. *(Pauses for a moment, then...)* Old rule out, new rule *in. (As he puts arm around INGA and squeezes her.)* Age does not count anymore. *(INGA giggles. to LOUELLA, indicating DEANNE.)* But you are still mother of beautiful daughter, yes?

LOUELLA. Yes, that's the truth, the whole truth and nothing but the truth.

MR.CHIU. Good. Now me and Inga we go eat. *(To INGA.)* You in the mood for Chinese?

INGA. *(Pinching his cheek.)* Inga always *in* mood for Chinese. *(They start to go.)*

MR.CHIU. *(To ROBERT.)* Tomorrow we have big meeting.

ROBERT. Good, good. How about ten AM ?

MR.CHIU. Too early. Big night tonight. How 'bout four PM ? It's good?

ROBERT. It's good.

(They all ad-lib 'goodbyes'.)

MR.CHIU. *(To INGA, shaking his head.)* Why they all switch names?

(INGA shrugs as ROBERT closes the door behind them.)

ROBERT. Well, that was a close one.

LOUELLA. I suppose I should be going.

ROBERT. *(To DEANNE.)* Why don't we drive your mother home?

LOUELLA. Don't be silly. I'll take the bus. It gives me a chance to practice my Spanglish.

DEANNE. *(To ROBERT.)* No, *you* take her. I still haven't read the paper.

ROBERT. *(To LOUELLA.)* Is that okay with you?

LOUELLA. If you insist.

ROBERT. Maybe I'll drop by the office for a few minutes on the way back.

LOUELLA. Adios. *(Kisses DEANNE on the cheek.)*

DEANNE. Bye.

ROBERT. See you later. *(Kisses DEANNE on the other cheek.)*

(They EXIT. DEANNE walks around, goes to the bed, picks up part of the Sunday Times, looks at it then tosses it back. She goes to the opposite wall and knocks three times.)

BLACKOUT

End of scene

Scene 3

(Several weeks later. Day.
DOORBELL.
After a few moments, DEANNE ENTERS from hallway, wearing a smock and holding a charcoal pencil.)

DEANNE. Coming!

(She opens front door. Standing there is BORIS, the mover.)

BORIS. Remember me?

DEANNE. Of course, Boris. What are you doing here?

BORIS. I just fall by to say hello. I am moving Mr. Day next door.

DEANNE. *(Surprised)* You are?

BORIS. He did not tell you?

DEANNE. Oh, sure. I just didn't know when exactly.

BORIS. Before this morning I think your brother is for real. *(Laughs)* Then he tell me everything.

DEANNE. *(Apprehensive)* Everything?

BORIS. He tell me he is *not* your brother. Well, I have to go. My partner downstairs freaking.

DEANNE. They finally got you a helper.

BORIS. A flake, but a helper. *(He starts to go.)*

DEANNE. By the way, how are things with you and your woman?

BORIS. Not so good.

DEANNE. I'm sorry to hear that.

BORIS. But I found someone else and Boris much happier.

DEANNE. That's nice. Well, thanks for dropping by and good luck.

BORIS. You too. Peace!

(He gives the 'peace' sign and EXITS. She closes door, starts walking toward hallway then turns around with determination, goes to front door and opens it. Standing there is SKIP.)

SKIP. I didn't even ring.

DEANNE. *(Covering)* I was just checking to see if Boris was still here.

SKIP. And I was just checking to see if *you* were still here. Can I come in?

DEANNE. I guess so.

SKIP. Did I catch you during work?

DEANNE. That's okay. *(Puts down her pencil on nearby surface.)* Why didn't you tell me you were moving today?

SKIP. Why? Were you planning to give me a going-away party?

DEANNE. No, but isn't it just good manners to tell

people who are part of your life...I mean, who *were* part of your life.

SKIP. I guess I didn't want to encumber you.

DEANNE. Encumber me? *(Laughs)* So where are you moving to?

SKIP. Back to the Village.

(DEANNE registers surprise.)

SKIP. *(CONT'D)* Yep. Right back where it all started for you and me.

DEANNE. I was under the impression that it started in college.

SKIP. It did. You didn't want to have anything to do with me at the time. It's hard to have a one-way love affair. Of course, when we ran into each other, a few years later, you came to your senses.

DEANNE. *(Laughs and taps him on the arm.)* You're impossible.

SKIP. That's me, the Impossible Music Man. Tell the truth, you really didn't like me very much when we first met.

DEANNE. You mean when I danced in your College Musical? I may not have liked you but I sure admired your talent. Everybody did. The girls were actually making bets as to how soon you'd have your first Broadway smash.

SKIP. I hope they didn't put too much money on that.

DEANNE. God, it all seems so long ago.

SKIP. And yet it's not.

DEANNE. Remember how we used to sneak into Broadway Musicals during intermission. Of course it only worked if they weren't hits.

SKIP. We sure saw a lot of bad 'half Musicals'.

DEANNE. Me, trying to peddle my designs around town.

SKIP. Til Avi Kaplan carne to the rescue.

DEANNE. Part-time.

SKIP. What about me, working at that awful piano bar on 34th Street?

DEANNE. But we had a lot of fun.

SKIP. And we had a lot of dreams.

DEANNE. We sure did. We were going to live in Paris.

SKIP. You were going to design for Dior or Chanel.

DEANNE. You were going to write songs for Charles Aznavour.

SKIP. That's before I found out he wrote his own songs. You were going to learn to cook.

DEANNE. And you were going to learn to dance. *(A beat.)* What about that place you had in the Village?

SKIP. You mean the one you liked so much that you moved in?

DEANNE. That apartment was so tiny you had to squeeze the piano into the bedroom.

SKIP. *Everything* was in the bedroom.

DEANNE. *(Laughs)* You had to sit on the bed to play.

SKIP. We both sat on the bed to play.

DEANNE. I'm talking about composing.

SKIP. You know, I still have that piano.

DEANNE. You mean that piano in there...*(Points to his apartment.)* is the same one?

SKIP. I don't dare get rid of it. It's my lucky piano. I'll bet you can't remember my first Network jingle?

(They look at each other and start to sing. SAMPLE #8 ON

DISC.)

DEANNE & SKIP.
COME DRIVE OUR VOLVO
SAFE AND QUIET VOLVO
GET BEHIND THE WHEEL
AND START TO FEEL
THAT VOLVO GO

(They laugh.)

DEANNE. *(Her laughter changes to sadness.)* Why did you have to go sell that other song to American Airlines? That was *my* song.

SKIP. It's still your song.

DEANNE. With those lyrics?

SKIP. I was working on new ones when you left me. *(A beat.)* I guess I didn't work fast enough.

DEANNE. And you didn't work hard enough either. You became complacent. You settled, you forgot about your gift.

SKIP. I know, I know. I did everything wrong.

DEANNE. *(A beat.)* I'm going to miss you, Skip. I won't miss your students but I'll miss you.

SKIP. I never stopped missing you. I've been missing you since the day you left me.

(The front door flies open and ROBERT rushes in.)

ROBERT. Deanne, I have stupendous news. *(Notices SKIP.)* Oh. *(To DEANNE.)* I just closed the deal with Chiu. We're going to be rich.

DEANNE. We *are* rich.

ROBERT. We're going to be richer. We must celebrate. We're going to need food and flowers and music...*(To SKIP.)* Are you available tonight? I'll pay you whatever you want. Name your price.

(SKIP looks over at DEANNE.)

DEANNE. Sure, why not?

SKIP. *(As he heads for door.)* Let's hope they haven't taken my piano yet. *(He runs out.)*

DEANNE. Congratulations.

ROBERT. Thanks. What does he mean, taken his piano?

DEANNE. He's moving.

ROBERT. Why? I thought he loved this building.

DEANNE. It's a complicated story.

ROBERT. If you say so. *(Back on subject.)* Do you want to invite your boss?

DEANNE. You think so?

ROBERT. Why not? And whomever else you might want.

DEANNE. What about mother?

ROBERT. I already spoke to her. *(Pacing excitedly.)* This Mr. Chiu is quite a character. He wants me to go back with him to Beijing for a few weeks. You know, meet all the other players. Do you have any desire to make that trip?

DEANNE. I don't think so, Robert. Besides I have a lot of work to do.

ROBERT. I don't see why you have to work at all. Well, you think about it, darling. I'm going to run in and take a shower.

(He heads for the hallway.)

DEANNE. *(Calls out.)* What kind of food should I order?

ROBERT. *(O.S.)* Guess!

(DEANNE gets her cell phone and dials.)

DEANNE. Is Mr. Kaplan there?...Deanne...Deanne Petridge. Are you new?...Oh, that's nice. Would you please tell him that I'm on the phone?...Thank you...Avi, get your party hat. Robert wants to celebrate...Robert, my husband ...Well, we're celebrating two things. Robert closed his China deal and mother found her Bergdorf-Goodman card...Yes, you can bring your new receptionist. Also tell Jovan he can bring someone too...Great. See you around eight. *(Hangs up, dials again.)* I'd like to order some food to go...oh, and make it extra spicy...

END OF SCENE

Scene 4

(Evening.
MUSIC CUE #9.
A number of balloons are visible. There are several coats strewn across the bed. Open umbrellas are resting on the floor. Party sounds emanate O.S., including SKIP's piano playing. It seems a good time is being had by all. The front door opens wide revealing a large sign that reads 'Come on in' as well as JOVAN accompanied by BORIS,

the mover. JOVAN is holding a closed wet umbrella.)

BORIS. I feel like I'm outa the loop here.

JOVAN. Don't be ridic. You know this apartment better than anyone.

BORIS. Does Mrs. Petridge know we are 'item'?

JOVAN. *(As he pinches BORIS'S cheek.)* You are so cute, calling us an item. Here, give me your coat.

(He helps BORIS off with his coat, then removes his own and throws both of them onto bed.)

BORIS. *(During the above.)* We are very late, no?

JOVAN. Better late than never. *(He starts toward hallway.)*

BORIS. What about umbrella?

JOVAN. You're right.

(He holds umbrella up, hits the button causing the umbrella to open with a pop, sending rain spray all over the room.)

JOVAN. *(CONT'D)* Think of it as rice.

(He takes BORIS by the arm as they start toward hallway to join the party just as INGA comes out of the guest bathroom.)

INGA. *(Extending her hand.)* Hi, I'm Inga.

JOVAN. *(Indicates BORIS.)* I'm Jovan and he's Boris.

INGA. Did you say Doris?

JOVAN. No, Boris. But Doris could,work.

INGA. *(Confused for a moment.)* Oh. By the way, this is

the only powder room you can use. The others are filled with flowers. At least, I think they are flowers. Are you friends of Skip or his neighbors?

JOVAN. Both. *(Indicates for her to go into hallway first.)* Shall we?

(JOVAN and BORIS follow. They are greeted O.S. by DEANNE, SKIP and AVI. The piano playing continues. A moment later DEANNE emerges followed by ROBERT. He has a drink in his hand.)

ROBERT. Dee, we need to talk.

DEANNE. Now? I was just running in to use the bathroom. Can't it wait?

ROBERT. I guess so.

(She ENTERS guest bathroom. LOUELLA appears from stage right hallway.)

LOUELLA. Well?

ROBERT. She's in the bathroom.

LOUELLA. Maybe you should wait till after the party. *(Taking out cigarettes.)* I need a smoke.

ROBERT. When did you start that?

LOUELLA. This morning. I need to practice.

(She heads for front door.)

LOUELLA. *(CONT' D)* You'd better get back in there. Mr. Chiu is getting bombed.

(She EXITS as she lights cigarette. We hear her coughing

O.S. ROBERT goes back to party. He bumps into AVI and GINA as they ENTER room.)
ROBERT. Having a good time, Avi?
GINA. Magnifico party.

(ROBERT disappears.)

GINA. *(CONT'D)* Avi, we should tell people we are engaged.
AVI. No!
GINA. But I want to boast about it.
AVI. Boast about it to me.

(DEANNE EXITS guest bathroom.)

DEANNE. You and Jeannine having fun?
GINA. *(Correcting her.)* It's *Gina!*
DEANNE. Sorry. How do you like your job as receptionist?
GINA. *(To AVI.)* Have you not told her? *(To DEANNE.)* I am also modelling on the side.
DEANNE. Really? Which side?
GINA. *(Confused)* I don't get it.
DEANNE. *(Indicating bathroom door.)* You can use it now.
GINA. I don't need to.
AVI. *(Pushing her along.)* Sure you do.

(GINA reluctantly goes into guest bathroom.)

AVI. *(Quietly)* Did I tell you Millie called?
DEANNE. Now what?

AVI. She decided not to go into business to compete with me.

DEANNE. So, does that mean that Moe is back?

AVI. Not only is my number one cutter back but there's even better news.

DEANNE. What?

AVI. Millie ran off with our Rabbi.

DEANNE. Oh my God! I hope he doesn't find out what she does at your Christmas parties.

AVI. It's okay, he's Reformed.

(They laugh. GINA comes out of bathroom.)

GINA. Well, that was a waste of time. I need a drink.

AVI. Me too.

DEANNE. Me too.

(Front door opens and LOUELLA ENTERS.)

LOUELLA. Me too.

(As AVI and GINA go back to party.)

DEANNE. Where were *you?*

LOUELLA. Down in the lobby with Fritz. He showed me how to blow smoke rings.

DEANNE. *(Appalled)* You're smoking?

LOUELLA. I'm nervous.

DEANNE. *(Sarcastic)* What happened? Did your 92nd Street Y membership run out?

LOUELLA. I happen to be interested in everything this

City has to offer. I'm just nervous this evening, that's all.

(They head back to party. Piano is still playing. Animated conversations and laughter continue O.S. MR. CHIU now appears. He has a drink in one hand and his cell phone in the other.)

(MR.CHIU. Speaks CHINESE for several moments into phone. Front door opens. Standing there is JEANNINE.)

JEANNINE. Am I too late for some fun?

MR.CHIU. *(Says a few quick words in Chinese and hangs up.)* No, you are right on time. I take your coat?

JEANNINE. Merci. Is that Skip playing?

MR.CHIU. You mean my protege. I am big investor in his show.

(He removes her coat, revealing that body of hers.)

MR.CHIU. *(CONT'D)* We are always looking for new faces. *(As he flips coat onto bed.)* And what do people call you?

JEANNINE. All sorts of names but I prefer Jeannine.

MR.CHIU. I prefer Jeannine too. Me, Sun Yun Chiu.

JEANNINE. *(Pokes him in the ribs.)* Me, some fun too. *(She laughs.)*

MR.CHIU. *(He laughs and indicates for her to go first.)* Apres-vous

(JEANNINE walks ahead, he follows. They disappear through hallway. Greetings, introductions, laughter continue O.S.

*as well as the piano playing. JOVAN appears. He's on his
cell phone. He's followed by an angry BORIS.)*

JOVAN. *(On phone.)* Yes...yes...

BORIS. You spend entire evening on the telephone. It
sucks.

JOVAN. *(On phone as he moves away from BORIS.)* Yes
...yes...*(Cups phone, whispers to BORIS.)* I'm almost done.

BORIS. *(Pointedly)* Yes, you are almost done.

JOVAN. *(On phone.)* Perfect. Tomorrow at five. *(Hangs
up.)* What's the matter with *you?*

BORIS. Oh? Now it's *my* bad?

JOVAN. Putting a Theatre piece together requires a great
many phone conversations.

BORIS. Maybe I hook up with wrong costume maker.

JOVAN. *(Going to him.)* Don't be ridic. We're having
our first spat, that's all. *(He holds his phone out in front of
them, smiles and snaps a photo.)* I want a picture of this for
posterity.

(Just then, INGA comes running in followed by MR. CHIU.)

MR.CHIU. I said I was sorry. So I call you Gina instead
of Inga. It's a normal mistake.

INGA. *(Indignant)* I'm a blonde, she is a black head.

*(JOVAN and BORIS sneak back into party as INGA walks
away from MR. CHIU.)*

MR.CHIU. I said I am sorry.

(INGA heads toward guest bathroom.)

MR.CHIU. *(CONT'D)* Where you going now?
INGA. To the loo.
MR.CHIU. *(Waves at her.)* Tooddleloo.

(She ENTERS guest bathroom and slams door shut. CELL PHONE rings. MR. CHIU checks his phone. It's not his. He starts looking through coats on bed. He's making a mess of things. Piano stops playing O.S.and recorded music takes over. MR. CHIU finally finds cell phone in pocket of coat. He answers it.)

MR.CHIU. Hello?...Hello? *(No answer.)*

(He takes it with him as he rushes back to party, bumping into SKIP holding an ice bucket.)

SKIP. We're running out of ice.
MR.CHIU. *(Holding up his glass.)* As long as you do not run out of scotch.

(SKIP EXITS apartment. INGA EXITS guest bathroom. INTERCOM buzzes. She goes to it and speaks.)

INGA. Hello?
INTERCOM VOICE. Your neighbors below you are starting to complain.
INGA. What about the ones above?
INTERCOM VOICE. You live on the top floor.
INGA. I never knew that. *(Hangs up.)*

(She starts toward hallway to rejoin party as DEANNE appears.)

DEANNE. Have you seen Skip?

INGA. *(Shakes her head.)* Maybe Skip skip out.

(SKIP ENTERS apartment with ice bucket.)

INGA. *(CONT'D)* See? Inga right.

(She disappears through hallway.)

DEANNE. Where'd you go?

SKIP. I went next door to get some ice. Technically it's still my place till tomorrow.

DEANNE. How are we going to handle this?

SKIP. I don't know. I also don't know how much longer I can pretend to be having a good time in there. Should I talk to Robert now?

DEANNE. Maybe I'd better do it.

(ROBERT and LOUELLA come walking in from party.)

LOUELLA. Oh, good, you're both here.

ROBERT. There's something we need to discuss.

SKIP. We have something to discuss too.

LOUELLA. *(To DEANNE.)* What your father...I mean, what your *husband* is saying...

DEANNE. I think we should go first.

SKIP. Yes, I agree.

ROBERT. Well, I happen to think *we* should go first.

LOUELLA. *(Jumping in, to DEANNE and SKIP.)* Bob's

right. It may affect what *you* want to say.

(DEANNE and SKIP look at one another.)

ROBERT. *(To DEANNE.)* This is very difficult. Firstly, because I'm your husband...

LOUELLA. And because I'm your mother.

(There's an awkward pause as all four look from one to the other.)

ROBERT. I think I may have done you a disservice when I married you.

DEANNE. What do you mean?

LOUELLA. Hear him out, dear.

ROBERT. Well, for one thing, I'm almost twice your age.

LOUELLA. Now don't exaggerate.

ROBERT. Which means we have different interests. For instance, I like to read the Wall Street Journal, you like Cosmo. I like Ballet, you like Broadway Shows. I like spending time at the Club and...well, more importantly, I think you're still in love with Skip.

(SKIP and DEANNE look at each other and smile sheepishly.)

ROBERT. *(CONT'D, to DEANNE.)* Now, perhaps you two can tell us what you want to talk about?

LOUELLA. *(To ROBERT.)* Why don't we finish our story first?

ROBERT. No, I'm curious. I'd like to hear what they

have to say.

DEANNE. *(Looking over at SKIP.)* We have something somewhat similar to discuss.

SKIP. The four of us are definitely in the same ballpark.

DEANNE. Maybe we should get right to the point, honey.

ROBERT. I think you just got to the point with that 'honey'.

SKIP. The truth is I never stopped loving Deanne.

LOUELLA. I knew it!

ROBERT. *(To DEANNE.)* And what about you?

DEANNE. Well, I did stop for awhile. But I guess not as long as I should have.

ROBERT. In other words, you stopped long enough to marry *me*.

LOUELLA. *(Reprimanding)* Robert!

DEANNE. No, he's entitled. *(To ROBERT.)* I suppose I was swept away by your success, your kindness, your maturity...In my own way, I *did* fall in love with you.

ROBERT. But...?

DEANNE. But I still loved this lazy bum here. *(Ruffles SKIP'S hair.)*

SKIP. *(Shrugs and smiles.)* That's me.

LOUELLA. *(To the three of them.)* I think it's all coming together very nicely, don't you?

SKIP. Yes, very nicely. I was prepared for a combination earthquake, hurricane, tsunami and Armageddon all rolled into one.

DEANNE. So, how do we work this all out?

ROBERT. Well, for starters, your mother and I will be going to china. *(To SKIP.)* On your airline, by the way.

LOUELLA. What are you kids going to do, stay in this place?

DEANNE. Skip got an apartment in the Village. Maybe he'll let me move in with him.

ROBERT. The Village? Isn't that filled with...

DEANNE. *(Cutting in.)* Interesting people of all persuasions.

(JEANNINE comes running in.)

JEANNINE. I am feeling very sick. *(To DEANNE.)* Forgive me but I accidentally flushed the flowers in the bathroom back there.

(She ENTERS guest bathroom.)

DEANNE. I suppose the two of you will be moving in here.

ROBERT. Your mother insists on living on the Westside. Apparently she has to be in walking distance to Mitzi Newhouse.

LOUELLA. And Whole Foods.

(JOVAN and BORIS walk in.)

JOVAN. So this is where everyone's hiding.

(He proceeds to find his coat as well as BORIS' on the bed during the following.)

DEANNE. You're leaving already?

JOVAN. Boris has an early call.

BORIS. I'm moving family of twelve from the burbs to a

loft in SoHo.

(JOVAN helps BORIS on with his coat.)

BORIS. *(CONT'D, to SKIP.)* I love your music. And I love your sister. She's hot.
SKIP. Thank you.
JOVAN. Remember me when it comes time for the costumes in your show. I don't plan to be part of the Jersey Theatre Scene forever.
BORIS. *(To JOVAN.)* What about umbrella?

(He reaches over and takes their umbrella.)

JOVAN. *(To others.)* He's so smart. Ciao!
SKIP. Ciao.

(All ad-lib 'goodnights' as the two of them EXIT.)

ROBERT. *(Quietly)* Yes, ciao.

(INTERCOM buzzes. SKIP is nearest. He answers.)

SKIP. Yes?
INTERCOM VOICE. There is a car here for some-young-Jew.
SKIP. That's Sun-Yun-Chiu!
INTERCOM VOICE. If you say so.
SKIP. He'll be right down. *(Hangs up.)* I'll go get him.

(SKIP heads for O.S. 'living room'.)

LOUELLA. I imagine, at some point, the four of us are going to have to sign some papers and stuff.

DEANNE. Should be simple enough. In a way, it's sort of like an exchange.

ROBERT. I'm sure solicitors will find ways to complicate matters.

(AVI and GINA ENTER.)

AVI. Thanks a lot, folks. Gina and I had a real good time. *(To GINA as he searches for their coats on bed.)* Didn't we, princess?

GINA. Yes, but we never told them our secret.

AVI. *(Grins)* That's why it's called a secret. *(To DEANNE as he helps GINA with her coat.)* The renovations at the shop are completed now. You can come work there if you'd like.

DEANNE. Thanks, Avi, but I think I'm going to keep working at home.

AVI. Let's go, Gina. You've got a big day tomorrow. A lot of phone calls to answer and a lot of tight dresses to try on.

GINA. I forget to tell Skip I will not be needing piano lessons for awhile.

AVI. I'm sure he'll manage.

(All ad-lib 'goodbyes' as AVI and GINA EXIT. SKIP returns with MR. CHIU who is a little tipsy.)

MR.CHIU. *(Looking through his pockets.)* I cannot find ticket for coat.

DEANNE. You don't have a ticket.

MR.CHIU. Then how will I get coat?

SKIP. It's okay. Just pick one you like.
MR.CHIU. I like that one.
(He grabs a lady's coat and starts putting it on)

LOUELLA. I'm afraid that's mine. How about this one?

(Holds up coat for him.)

(MR. CHIU struggles with coat as he tries to put arms into sleeves.)

MR.CHIU. *(During above.)* This was best party I ever go to in America. Also only one. *(Laughs, then to DEANNE.)* So, I see you soon in Beijing?
DEANNE. Not exactly. My mother is going to stand in for me.
MR.CHIU. You are very kind daughter to give free trip to mother.

(JEANNINE comes out of guest bathroom, feeling much better now. MR. CHIU spots her.)

MR.CHIU. Come, we go now.
JEANNINE. But I'm not...*(Thinks about it for a moment.)* Okay, we go.

(Takes Mr. CHIU'S arm.)

MR.CHIU. *(To SKIP.)* Do not forget. Now that I have money in Musical, Sun Yun expects to see many girls in show. Goodbye everybody!

(He and JEANNINE EXIT as others ad-lib 'goodbyes' etc.)

LOUELLA. *(To ROBERT.)* Do you think he's going to take her to China?

ROBERT. I have no idea. He's the most baffling businessman I've ever encountered.

(INGA ENTERS from hallway. She's on her cell phone.)

INGA. I don't understand a word you are saying. *(Cups phone.)* Some Chinese woman keeps calling me. *(Into phone.)* Sorry. *(Hangs up.)* I think maybe I take Mr. Chiu's phone by mistake. *(Looks around.)* Where is Sun Yun?

DEANNE. He just left...with you.

INGA. *(Confused, then...)* He left? *(Starts to run out.)* Thank you all very much. *(To Skip.)* Cancel singing lessons ...perhaps forever! (She EXITS.)

ROBERT. Well, I imagine we should be going as well.

(Takes out his cell phone and dials.)

LOUELLA. *(To DEANNE.)* Can we help you clean up?

DEANNE. No thanks, we'll be fine.

ROBERT. *(Into phone.)* Would you bring the car around, please? *(Hangs up.)*

LOUELLA. *(To DEANNE.)* Call me in the morning...but not too early. *(Kisses her on cheek.)*

(SKIP steps forward awkwardly and kisses LOUELLA on cheek.)

SKIP. Have a great trip.

LOUELLA. Thank you.

(SKIP goes over to ROBERT even more awkwardly, extends his hand. They shake.)

SKIP. I hope we can all laugh about this someday.

ROBERT. *(Flashes a wide smile.)* We're laughing now.

(DEANNE walks LOUELLA and ROBERT to the door.)

DEANNE. *(Notices open umbrella on floor.)* Someone forgot their umbrella.

LOUELLA. I'll take it. *(Grabs it.)* It might be the rainy season in China.

DEANNE. *(To ROBERT.)* Is there anything you need from here? You know, shaving stuff, pajamas?...

LOUELLA. He's got that at my place.

(DEANNE and SKIP look at each other, impressed.)

DEANNE. *(To ROBERT.)* This is a little awkward but thanks for everything.

*(She kisses him on the cheek, warmly.
They are all at the front door. Phone RINGS. All four reach for their cell phones. All answer at the same time.)*

DEANNE SKIP LOUELLA & ROBERT. *(In unison.)* Hello?

(It's the phone next to the bed. They all put their cell phones

away as DEANNE answers it.)

DEANNE. *(Into phone.)* Who?...You live downstairs?...I know, I apologize. Next time I promise we'll invite you. *(Hangs up.)*

(All four ad-lib 'goodnights', 'good lucks' etc. ROBERT and LOUELLA EXIT. DEANNE rips notice off front door then closes it. She and SKIP embrace.)

DEANNE. Phew! *(They kiss.)*
SKIP. Close your eyes. I have a surprise for you.

(He walks toward hallway.)

DEANNE. *(Covers her eyes.)* The last time I closed my eyes I wound up in here with a new husband.
SKIP. *(As he goes toward hallway.)* Well this time you're winding up with an old husband and, with any luck at all, maybe even a baby.

(A wide smile crosses her face as he disappears through hallway. The recorded background music is turned off. This is followed by the sound of squeaking wheels approaching.)

SKIP. *(CONT'D, O.S., calls out.)* I think I'm going to need your help!
DEANNE. I'm going to have to look.

(She opens her eyes and joins him O.S.)

DEANNE. *(CONT'D, O.S.)* What are you doing?
(The squeaking wheels continue. The upright piano appears
with the two of them maneuvering it into 'bedroom'.)

DEANNE. *(CONT'D)* Where are you going to put it,
back next door?
SKIP. Nope. *(As he places it so that the keys are not*
visible to audience.) We're going to leave it in here, where it
belongs.

(He sits on the bed and begins playing the 'American Airlines'
melody. MUSIC CUE #11. SAMPLE #10 ON DISC.)

SKIP. *(CONT'D)* I wrote some new lyrics.
(Sings and plays.)
I'M THROUGH WITH WORDS OF LOVE
FOR SOAPS AND CARS
I'M BACK TO MOON
AND JUNE AND SOFT GUITARS

SO LONG TO HAIR THAT FLOWS
AND LIPS THAT SHINE
GOODBYE TO BEERS WITH LIME
I FOUND MY WAY

AND AS FOR FRIENDLY SKIES
I SAY ADIEU
I'LL SHARE MY NEW FOUND HIGHS
WITH YOU, ANEW

FAREWELL TO WASTED RHYMES
AND WASTED NIGHTS
THANKS TO THOSE HARBOR LIGHTS
I FOUND MY WAY

 DEANNE & SKIP.
TOGETHER
UNTIL DEATH DO US PART
THIS TIME LET'S NOT JUST DREAM IT
LET'S REALLY MEAN IT
WE FOUND OUR WAY
WE FOUND OUR WAY
WE FOUND OUR WAY

(They kiss. MUSIC CUE #12.)

FINAL CURTAIN

PROPERTY PLOT

ACT 1 - Scene 1
Dolly
Mattress
Sofa
Cell phone
Small gift wrapped box (bagles inside)
Several lamps (matching)
Female-form mannequin
Bouquet of flowers
Living room chair
Large bird cage
Several small tables
Large envelope (holds dress designs)
Large flat TV
Several large cardboard boxes

ACT 1 - Scene 2
Boxes have been removed
Mattress now has sheets, bedspread and pillows
Lamps have been placed on either side of bed on night tables
Men's silk bathrobe
Neatly pressed pajamas
Business Week magazine
Negligee
Sheer robe

ACT I - Scene 3
Stuffed chair Tables Lamps
Large armoire More boxes

ACT 11 - Scene 1
Bed and ned frame
Large flat TV on wall
Paintings
Rug
More furniture
Lamps
Chairs
Bureau

ACT 11 - Scene 2
TV remote Yoga mat Shawl

ACT 11 - Scene 3
Smock Charcoal pencil

ACT 11 - Scene 4
Balloons
Coats on bed
Open umbrellas on floor
Wet closed umbrella
Cigarette
Lighter
Glass of scotch on the rocks
Mr. Chiu's cell phone
Jovan's cell phone
Another cell phone in pocket of coat on bed
Ice bucket
Inga's cell phone
Robert's cell phone

Skip's cell phone
Louella's cell phone
Old upright piano on wheels

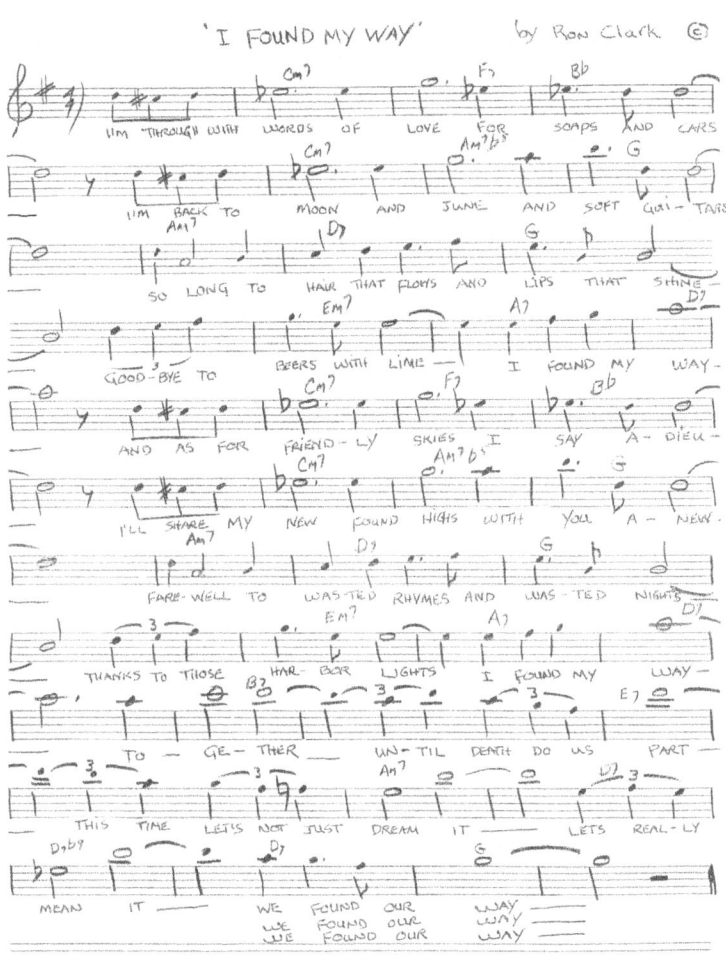

'I FOUND MY WAY' by Ron Clark ©

I'm through with words of love for soaps and cars

I'm back to moon and june and soft guitars

So long to hair that flows and lips that shine

Good-bye to beers with lime — I found my way —

And as for friendly skies I say adieu —

I'll share my new found highs with you anew.

Farewell to wasted rhymes and wasted nights

Thanks to those harbor lights I found my way —

Together until death do us part —

This time let's not just dream it lets really

Mean it — We found our way —
We found our way —
We found our way —

AUGUSTUS MUSIC PUBLISHING   ASCAP   e-mail -
9720 WILSHIRE BLVD, SUITE 300   augustusmusicpub @ earthlink. net
BEVERLY HILLS, CA 90212

OTHER TITLES AVAILABLE FROM SAMUEL FRENCH

NORMAN, IS THAT YOU?

Ron Clark and Sam Bobrick

Full Length, Comedy / 3m, 2f / Int.

Don Knotts starred in the wildly successful Kansas City premiere of a revised and updated version of this perennial favorite that originally starred Lou Jacobi and Maureen Stapleton on Broadway. A dry cleaner from Ohio arrives in New York to visit his adult son Norman after his wife runs off with his own brother. Instead of the solace he is expecting, he finds more turmoil when he discovers his son is living with Garson, a male partner. The irascible and stubborn father struggles comically with his denial of Norman's orientation and his begrudging respect for Garson, even seeking out a lady of the night to set Norman straight. In the end, this loving father comes face to face with his affection for his son and his wife, who shows up repentant in New York. Love and hilarity triumph.

"This is a new, radical rewrite [that] revolves around a realistic, caring portrayal of a gay man and his parents.... Funny and ultimately affecting."
– *The Kansas City Star*

"One laugh after another.... It doesn't get any better."
– *Kansas City Kansan*

"A funny play ... about values, love and human behavior."
– KC Alive

"It's funny . . . yards and yards of solid laughs."
– ABC TV
SAMUELFRENCH.COM

www.ingramcontent.com/pod-product-compliance
Lightning Source LLC
Chambersburg PA
CBHW070632120726
47909CB00004B/1408